MARK of ETERNITY

MARK of ETERNITY

ZACHARY MOULDER

To request permissions or get into contact:
zachary.d.moulder@gmail.com

Edited by C.K. Korfo
Illustrations and cover by Doan Trang

ISBN (paperback) 978-0-6456163-0-9
ISBN (ebook) 978-0-6456163-1-6

Dedicated to our Lord for the gift of life
and to my friends and family for making it worth living.

CHAPTER ONE

'Quick! The storm's almost over us!'

'Hurry, Eve, hurry!'

Eve ran as fast as she could along a tight, barren mountain trail, leaping over rocks and sliding down loose patches of gravel and ice. She gasped for air, but her intake was bottlenecked by the decrepit gasmask that was strapped to her face. It flexed and shrank with her breaths as it pulled in the toxic air, filtering out the ingredients that would spell a slow and painful death, and spat out stale, but breathable air for her use.

It was dark, almost pitch black. Overhead, thick dark clouds blocked out a perpetual starry night sky, threatening to unleash their devastating deluge. Strong winds had kicked up swarms of razor-sharp rocks that macerated themselves against each other to form a suffocating cloud of deafening dust that whipped against Eve's feeble frame.

The dust mixed with the beads of sweat that waterfalled down her entire body, the thick cold-weather clothing that made operating in this environment possible now trapping her body heat and cooking her from the inside out. She winced as thousands of microscopic pieces of rock tore into the exposed portions of her face, making dozens of tiny bloody lacerations that were clogged in quick succession by more dust. Her eyes watered, some dust managing to seep into the cracks of her goggles, reducing her vision to little more than what her shoulder-mounted flashlight could illuminate.

Two figures ran ahead—her mother and father. Their larger builds were barely influenced by the gales that knocked Eve around and they were beginning to pull further ahead.

'I can't run any faster!' Eve called out to them. A gust of wind rattled her balance, but she managed to stabilise herself.

'Come on, Eve! Not far now!' Nisma, Eve's mother, shouted from somewhere within the dust cloud.

Eve could feel her head going faint. 'I-I can't!' she yelled, her voice hoarse.

'Nearly there, Eve! Let's go!' Eve's father, Eli, called back.

Eve swallowed and fought to regain her focus. She approached a spot in the trail where the mountain walls closed in considerably to form a tight crevice. She slowed and slid her way through sideways, grabbing the walls with gloved hands and pulling herself along. Pointed stone talons tore into her, ripping shreds of clothing and garments and tossing them into the breeze. Eve winced and groaned when a particularly devious shard of rock sliced through every layer of clothing and claimed a section of her back. She fought through to the other side, ignoring the rapidly growing pool of blood that was soaking into her jackets and pants. The sensation was short lived as the sub-zero temperatures of the air nipped at her exposed skin and flash froze her blood to her body, stopping the bleeding.

'Mom! Dad! Wait!' she shouted out, keeping a hand firmly planted against her mask and another pressed up to the laceration on her back.

There was no response from her parents. When she broke through to the other side and the trail widened again, Eve took off in hopes of catching up. She followed the trail for some time, her flashlight catching the occasional glimpse of humanoid figures that told her she was still on track.

'Come on, Eve!' someone called back to her.

The wind was too fierce for Eve to determine who'd said it, and they sounded much further away than she had anticipated. She increased her pace to a sprint, pumping her arms and sucking in as much air as her mask would allow. Eve paid little attention to the ground before her, focussing instead on trying to locate the source of the voice. Her foot landed on a loose rock, kicking it out from underneath her. She felt her ankle bend in an unnatural way before it snapped under her weight. A piercing pain shot up her leg, and Eve screeched as she fell to the ground hard. Jagged rocks dug into her face and body, tearing flesh away as she reeled in pain. Her mask was knocked loose, and she choked as the toxic atmosphere seeped in and ate at her from the inside out.

Eve was slow to rise, the pain in her ankle and the countless cuts and bruises made her body feel like it was on fire. Gritting her teeth, she stammered to her feet and rested on her one good foot. She sealed her mask back up, mustered up all of the remaining air in her lungs and exhaled as powerfully as possible while she held a hand over the intakes of her filter. The outlet valves allowed the air to exit back into the atmosphere, evacuating most of the toxins that had found their way in. Eve removed her hand off the filter and took a deep breath, taking in the serviceable air.

Her breathing problem solved, Eve continued on along the trail. Her progress was slow, and she could not help but feel that she had fallen too far behind. She winced every time her injured foot struck the ground and sent a pulse of pain up her leg. A ball of phlegm rose up in her throat, and she spat it out into her mask; it tasted metallic.

'Wait for me!' she called out into the dust clouds. There was no response, but Eve could feel the wind dying down and a break in the dust further up the trail. *They must already be at the top,* she deduced. Knowing the end was near, she mustered the last of her strength and pushed onwards through the slackening winds to the top of the trail to the Outlook.

Before long a pause in the storm swept over Eve, and she slowed. Relief washed over her as the buffeting effects of the dust dissipated and her vision improved. A giant cone structure morphed into shape from the dust, at least twenty metres tall and pointed straight up towards the sky.

As Eve drew near, details began to materialise on its matte-grey form. Piping. Portholes. Ladders. Thrusters. A bold '7' was posted on its sole door, which was held open against the wind by hydraulics, and a series of tubes and cables hung off of dozens of places and fed into machinery mounted on the ground around it. In a previous life, it was an escape pod but, after years of modifications it took on a new role and became known simply as the Rocket.

About fifty metres from the Rocket, and two hundred from Eve, the figures of her parents approached it at considerable speed.

'Wait!' Eve shouted out to them with a cough, more blood rising up out of her injured lungs.

The wind must have carried her voice away with it as her parents did not falter in their advance. Eve shook her head and resumed her hobbling at as best of a pace as possible. She watched as her parents reached the Rocket and split off from each other, taking pipes and couplings off of its structure. Once all of the links had been severed, they ascended a ladder and passed through the open '7' door.

'Wait! Stop! Don't go!'

They did not answer. Eve did not even see them look in her general direction. They ascended a ladder on the Rocket's chassis and closed the door behind them, sealing them in from the outside world.

Despite her injuries, Eve crossed the distance leading up to the Rocket in quick succession, and she now stood before the towering construction. Gases vented from numerous openings across it. Bits and pieces of metal flexed on hydraulic joints. A low rumbling began to sound from the thrusters beneath it. Eve's eyes widened. *They're going to launch!* She forced her way up the ladder, groaning as she felt her ankle bend and grind against itself. Putting her face up against the door's porthole, Eve hammered as hard as she could. She watched her parents inside, her mother at the flight controls and her father in the co-pilot seat, go through the pre-launch checks. They could not hear her. Or maybe they did not listen.

'Please!' Eve screamed, desperation sinking in. 'Open the door! Let me in!'

She watched as Nisma plant a finger on a prominent button on the console before her. In an instant the thrusters beneath the Rocket burst into life and sent a plume of dust and smoke out from the ground. Eve held on as tight as she could, but was thrown off with a scream by the shuddering machine.

She fell to the ground hard, feeling several more breaks that resonated pain all through her body. The Rocket rose up into the sky like an ascending star, its flames licking at the ground as if it defied gravity. Eve found herself caught in the backblast.

Superheated air scorched her clothes, melting them to her body, before a strong thrust of dust and dirt sent her rolling across the ground. She came to rest against a small rocky outcrop.

Eve coughed as she took in the outside air and watched helplessly as the Rocket rose further up into the sky. Blood spluttered out her mouth and dribbled down her chin. Her face was burnt beyond recognition, some parts down to the bone, and her clothes were now a molten mass of material that clung to her body like tumours. She was in such tremendous pain that she could barely form simple thoughts. She looked up at the sky and traced the Rocket as it grew smaller and smaller with every passing second until it disappeared into the clouds. She struggled to speak, her vocal cords now burnt beyond functionality and her lungs either singed or being eaten up by the atmosphere with each laboured breath.

'Mommy. Daddy. Please don't go,' she managed to utter, a tear welling from her eye. 'Don't leave me.'

A droplet landed beside her and ate away a small hole in the rock around it, emitting a noxious cloud of gas as it did so. This was followed by another droplet, then another. Before long, it was raining all around Eve as the sky showed sympathy for her anguish and wept with her.

She held her hand up to cover her eyes. A droplet landed on it, burning a hole straight through it in an instant. Eve dropped her hand and lay there as the Rain began to land on her broken body and eat away at her flesh. She did not give a reaction to it, not a sound; her body was already far too gone to be saved. She merely remained there, feeling herself be disassembled by her very atoms until she finally accepted the embrace of the perpetual night and became one with the world.

A repeating, monotonous wail filtered into Eve's ears and pulled her into consciousness. She felt the coarse, jagged rocks beneath her morph into a familiar soft mattress that formed and supported the shape of her body. Her thick environmental clothing was now a heavy blanket draped over her, and her mask was a well-acquainted pillow that she had buried her face into.

Sweat drenched her face and body, and Eve could feel the heat underneath the blanket reaching an uncomfortable level. She stirred, tugging at the blanket and throwing off to the side. Cool, stale air sapped at her body heat, its effects exacerbated by her sweat and thin monochromatic sleepwear.

Eve groaned and opened an eye, examining her surroundings. She was in a room, her bedroom. Small. Four walls, a roof and a floor; all made of the same patchwork of utilitarian pipelines and metal sheeting. A beam of white light blazed through a modest porthole from outside and illuminated the entire space. Eve lay in a single bed, the bottom half of a bunk that was built into one of the walls.

A desk and chair formed the opposing wall, and a closed hydraulic steel door stood perpendicular beside them. The desk was littered with bits and pieces of electronics and cablings that spilled over onto the floor and even up into the top bed of the bunk like a vagrant mould infestation. At the epicentre, atop a mountain of components on the desk, was an idle robotic head.

A blinking light from her desk caught Eve's eye. A petite computer screeched with an almost ear-splitting tone. She tutted and rose from her bed to her feet, stopping to take a glance out of the porthole on her way. It was bright outside, the result of several flood lights being powered by a grumbling generator. Their light drenched everything, revealing smooth cave walls potted with signs of recent excavation and expansion.

Stalactites and stalagmites lined the darker realms of the cave, the last remnants of hundreds that had been knocked down and disposed of to make space. They cast long shadows out into the abyss beyond the reach of the flood lights; the edge of the eternal night that existed beyond the boundaries that light set.

In the centre of it all, and only fifty metres from Eve's porthole, was a familiar cone-like structure that was laid on its side atop a ramshackle mobile launch platform. Dozens of cables and tubes linked up to it and ran down to the ground to the supporting machinery. The Rocket was still here; there would be no launch today.

Eve pulled herself away from the porthole and turned her attention to her desk where the increasingly irritating wailing continued to sound. Head still dizzy from sleep, she stumbled over to her chair and sat down and shifted from components to the side to free the computer. A tap of a button on the keyboard silenced the wails, and Eve's room returned to silent tranquillity. It took a moment for the computer to wake up, and Eve's eye wandered over to a framed photograph beside the computer's monitor.

It depicted a cheerful Eve, barely a cycle over five years old, Nisma smiling coolly, but no doubt worrying beyond reason beneath her facade and Eli grinning from ear to ear with a thumbs-up and a hand rubbing through Eve's hair. They all stood before a smoking wreck which would, one day, become the Rocket. Eve remembered it well; it was only a few years ago. She felt a sense of calm wash over her, removing the last of the anxiety caused by her nightmare. *Just a bad dream,* she mentally concluded. *Nothing to worry about.*

The monitor blinked to life, displaying several diagnostic programs and dozens of lines of code. Tapping away with the mouse, Eve closed some of the programs after glossing over them. She paused when she reached a program labelled 'SPUD OS' that flashed a full upload bar with 'Upload Complete' displayed beneath it.

Eve smiled. 'Done already, huh?'

She sifted through the electronics beneath the robotic head and retrieved a humble motherboard. With a flip of a switch, power surged through the circuitry. Systems engaged, indicator bulbs illuminated, cooling fans whirred up to maximum revolutions and solid-state drives clicked and clacked with thousands of calculations a second.

'Let's see if you'll work *this* time, Spud,' Eve said, taking up the robotic head with both hands. She rubbed a thumb across one of Spud's idle optics, cleaning some dust away. 'You can do it, buddy.'

A droning buzz popped from the electronics, and a small plume of smoke rose up from the pile. In an instant everything shut down. Fans slowed to a halt, and drives stopped clacking.

Eve dropped Spud's head onto the desk and slumped back in her chair with a sigh. She sniffed at the air and caught the familiar scent of fried electronics. She rubbed her eyes, frustrated. 'Dammit.'

'Eve? You awake?' Nisma called from outside. 'Breakfast is ready.'

The common room, at least that was what the schematics called it, was a large area designed for socialising and conversing with others who also inhabited the all-environment, atmospherically sealed vehicle. It was one of several cubicles that were heartily categorised as rooms. There were two bedrooms. One for Eve and the other for her parents that both led straight into the common room. There used to be more, but they have long since been converted to storage areas or workspaces.

There was the medbay, which served the function that its name suggested. Thankfully, not very often. It opened out into the common room and was wedged in between Eve and her parents' bedrooms. It was also the only room sufficiently soundproofed. A stairwell towards the frontal side of the common room ascended up to the cockpit where the vehicle could be controlled as well as a seldom-used ancillary airlock that granted access out onto the roof.

A ladder beside the stairs descended down into the belly of the vehicle where a large cargo bay containing smaller vehicles, storage containers, water tanks, supplies, a crane and more are kept. In a former life, of an age and place lost far away into the past, this marvellous creation probably had a name and a purpose with meaning behind it. Today it is simply called the Rover, and it was Eve's home.

Eve and her parents sat at a round dining table built into the floor in the centre of the common room. Originally made to seat twelve, the nine unneeded chairs had long since been torn up and thrown out to save space and weight, leaving the remaining three with almost even spacing between them. If the dining table were an analogue clock, Eve would be at the six 'o'clock position, Nisma at two and Eli at ten.

9:50 more like, Eve corrected in her head, remembering the manufacturing defect in Eli's chair that positioned him ever so slightly closer to her—a factor that irritated her mother's obsessive nature to no end.

They each had a serving of baked potato and cooked fish before them, the most recent harvest from the large aquaponics tank housed below in the storage area, sided with a glass of recycled water and a dose of multivitamins and supplements. Eve picked at her food, pondering how she could rectify her electrical dilemma. Eli was also deep in thought and had a look that rang of nostalgia. Though, what he could have been thinking about was beyond anyone but himself.

Nisma gave Eli a sideways glance. 'So, I figured out what was wrong with the Rocket's console,' she said, performing a neat bisection of a potato with her knife and popping it into her mouth with her fork. She chewed quietly, waiting for Eli to respond, her curly black hair bobbing on her shoulders as she did so. She had an unassuming build, slightly on the heavier side. She wore a modest black and white jumpsuit similar to what Eve and Eli also wore. Her brown eyes, a shade darker than her tanned complexion, regarded Eli intently.

Eli was the polar opposite of Nisma; short blond hair, fair complexion, deep-blue eyes and a stubble. He was built strong with broad shoulders. He often touted his time as a sports player, perhaps that was what he was thinking of?

That just left Eve, who was a hybrid of the two. She had a light prepubescent build. Her skin was lighter than Nisma's, but darker than Eli's. She had black hair like her mother's, but it was straight like her father's. Her eyes were the same as Nisma's, however. Something about alleles.

'Do tell,' Eli grunted, his face hinting that he was still deep in thought.

'It's been fried, through and through,' Nisma said bluntly, swallowing her tuber. 'Must have happened when we forced it to eject.'

'Hence why it wouldn't turn on?' Eli asked, pulling free of his internal affairs and raising his head ever so slightly.

Nisma pointed a finger justly. 'Exactly.'

Eli nodded, giving Nisma a 'told you so' look. 'What about the rest of the Rocket?'

Nisma shrugged, evidently not caring for Eli's silent jab. 'Don't know. Can't test it if I can't turn it on first, right?'

'Right,' Eli mumbled, his mind drifting back inwards.

Nisma leaned in close to him and spoke in a hushed tone, as if to not draw Eve's attention. 'We can go to the *Eternity* today. I'm sure there'll be *more* consoles on board we can scavenge.'

Eli simply nodded. 'Sounds good.'

The *Eternity* was the name of a colossal generation shipwreck only a few kilometres from the cave. Its name hinted at its purpose—to carry a large population on a journey across the void between the stars over several thousands of years. Its place of origin, Earth. Its destination, Concord Prime, which it had succeeded a decade prior after over ten thousand years adrift in deep space.

But that was where the good times had ended. The scans that had initially held Concord Prime as an attractive subject for human colonisation proved to be wrong. It was a barren wasteland devoid of all life and home to a devastating acidic weather phenomenon known simply as the Rain. Its orbit aligned perfectly with its axial rotation, giving one side an eternal day of searing heat and molten lava and the other a perpetual night of sub-zero temperatures and rolling, frozen hills. Its atmosphere was totally unbreathable for humans without the appropriate equipment.

Concord Prime had proved to be the epitome of hell and that was before the crash. Left with no means to return home, the crew of the *Eternity* attempted to land in the small temperate zone between the two polarised halves of the tortured world. They failed and the *Eternity* crashed several hundred kilometres within the night side. Killing all but three.

Eve was not alive to witness it, Nisma still being several months pregnant with her at the time of the incident, and every attempt she had made at extracting an answer as to how they had escaped with their lives was always quickly shot down. All she knew was, shortly after the crash, her parents found the Rover, the last of its kind in working order, and fled the unstable wreck not to return until the cacophony of explosions and erratic radiation spikes calmed down and made short scavenging trips inside viable. Eve would emerge into their new world shortly after as the first, and subsequently only, child of Concord.

'All right, we'll head there after breakfast,' Nisma concluded, taking up another piece of potato. 'You don't have anything you need to do today, do you?'

Eli shook his head; Eve could tell he was not overly keen. 'No, I'm free. There should be some consoles on the bridge, anyway.'

He glanced over to Eve and changed the subject. 'So, Eve.'

'Hm?' Eve grunted, not expecting to be put on the spot.

She raised her head and her eyes bounced between her mother and father. *Did I do something?*

'How's your project going?' Eli asked with a smile.

'Oh,' Eve said, thankful she was not in trouble for once. 'I had the self-learning program uploaded during rest period but, when I fired it up earlier, the processor shorted out. I think it had too much power drawn through it.'

'I see,' Eli nodded, tapping his chin, 'Got any spares?'

Eve shook her head. She was half expecting him to provide the token 'turn it off and on again' proposal that he had offered several times in the past. She often humoured him when he did, knowing full well that his knowledge in the field of detailed electronics and software were severely lacking, something she would occasionally jab back at in good spirit. 'That was the last one,' she said bluntly, idly picking at her food. 'I've looked all over the Rover for a spare.'

'Right, right,' Eli tutted, scratching at his stubble. He glanced at Nisma, who already had a stern look on her face. Eli grinned and turned back to Eve. 'Tell you what, Eve,' he started, leaning in as if he were about to make a deal of a lifetime. 'While I'm looking for that new console for your mother in the *Eternity*, *you* can scavenge around for any loose processors we might find along the way. How's that sound?'

Eve's eyes lit up. She had never been inside the *Eternity* before, always having been relegated to staying inside the Rover with her mother while Eli explored on his own. He had told her many stories of that great wreck and brought back countless trinkets and doo-dads for her builds. Not to mention the tales of the lives lived before the crash. *How great it must have been.*

'Really? Thanks, Dad!'

Eli could not help but smile. 'No worries, kiddo.'

He glanced back to Nisma with a smirk. She burned a pair of holes through his skull.

CHAPTER TWO

The remnants of the *Eternity* lay scattered hundreds of kilometres across Concord Prime's tormented surface with the majority of the wreck having come to a rest atop a modest range of hills that had long since been eaten away by the Rain from their original splendour. Eve recalled Nisma likening the wreck of the *Eternity* to a sunken corpse of a great fish that swam the oceans of their distant home world. She could not recall the name of the fish, or properly picture what an ocean would look like for that matter, but the comparison managed to linger in her mind nonetheless.

Eve had studied the schematics of the *Eternity* extensively. Learning that, when it was in one piece, it was over twenty kilometres long and almost a kilometre in diameter. It housed hundreds of levels, dozens of sectors and all manner of facilities, most of which Eve could not imagine being useful in any meaningful sense outside of making life in the void slightly more bearable.

The Rover approached the side of the *Eternity* along a ridgeline on one of the hills the great vessel lay upon. Its form dwarfed the Rover, making it look no more significant than a pebble beside a boulder. The view of the ship was breathtaking no matter how many times Eve saw it. She and her parents were inside the cockpit—Nisma at the helm, Eli standing beside her and Eve leaning against the door out into the common room behind them. She watched the immense form of the *Eternity* draw ever closer in the cockpit windows as Nisma guided the trundling wheels of the Rover down a well-trodden path into its great shadow. *To think that this was created by people like us,* Eve thought, eyes straining to pick out the finer details of the wreck.

Eve looked up and saw the starry sky filled with flickering lights. A large white object, horrifically scarred like the planet it orbited, hung ominously among the little twinkling stars and bathed the world in its silvery splendour; Concord Minor, or Minor for short, Concord Prime's sole moon. Its shape used to be circular, but a cataclysmic disaster in aeons past had fractured the great celestial body, leaving hundreds of fragments to orbit the chunk that remained. These fragments would often fall down upon Concord Prime in a shower of flaming meteors that would give light to a world otherwise stuck in perpetual darkness. Eve always found it beautiful whenever Minor rained on Concord Prime, but was secretly thankful that she was never anywhere near where the fragments were impacting.

Eve watched Minor vanish behind the *Eternity* as the Rover passed into its shadow and advanced towards a large opening in its structure, slowing to a halt with gears grinding and suspension squeaking in protest. Nisma pressed a few buttons and flipped a few levers to begin the shutdown sequence.

Eli patted Eve on the shoulder, tearing her attention away from the ship that now enveloped them. His face was clean shaven and visibly smooth. 'Let's go,' he said, smiling as he headed for the stairs to the common room.

Eve nodded, her excitement almost boiling over as she followed. A hand grabbed onto her arm before she could make it to the stairs. She looked back and met Nisma's sombre eyes. There was a moment's silence where only the sound of Eli's fading footsteps passed between Eve and her mother.

'You be careful out there,' Nisma eventually snarled, her tone making Eve feel slightly uneasy.

'I will, Mom.' Eve nodded, trying to politely pull free of her mother's grasp.

'You stick with your father,' Nisma ordered, 'and *keep* your radio on.'

Her severity made Eve's anxiety skyrocket. She simply nodded again, hoping it would please her mother. Nisma released her grip on her and let Eve join Eli downstairs.

The airlock was tight, definitely not made for two people. Eve and Eli shuffled about inside the claustrophobic chamber as they donned their equipment. First came several layers of thick synthetic cold-weather clothing that hung from a series of hooks built into the wall, then their bags and rucksacks containing water, rations, filters, batteries and more. Lastly, their masks, goggles and gloves. It was heavy, and Eve struggled to get any form of decent mobility and dexterity under all the weight she now bore, but it was a necessity when one worked out in the forbidding environment of Concord Prime.

'Got enough layers?' Eli asked, purging his mask and completing the seal against his face.

'Yep,' Eve replied, fastening her sleeves around her wrists. She was already working up a sweat underneath all her clothes.

'Flashlight working?' Eli inquired, flicking the light on his shoulder on and off in Eve's face.

Eve giggled and did the same back. 'Yep.'

'Mask and goggles fit properly?'

Eve nodded, feeling at her mask. 'Yep.'

She got a sense of déjà vu as her nightmare flashed back to her mind for a split second then vanished as quickly as it came. *Just a dream, Eve,* she told herself.

'Radio?' Eli asked, tapping at an earpiece in his ear.

Eve nodded, tapping at her own. 'Yep.'

Eli held up a mask filter before dropping it into his bag. 'Spare filters?'

Eve jingled her rucksack and felt several filters clack against each other. 'Yep.'

Eli smiled. 'Awesome.'

He pressed a button on a large wrist watch. 'You got me, Nis?' he said, his voice echoing in Eve's earpiece.

Nisma's voice sounded back, 'Loud and clear. Your locators are operational, too.'

'As if I'd get lost,' Eli tutted, raising an eyebrow at Eve who suppressed a giggle.

'Wouldn't be the first time,' Nisma responded, thick with sarcasm.

'How's it looking out there?' Eli asked, changing the subject.

'There's a few clouds, but little chance of Rain. Temperature's hovering around negative twenty.'

A normal weather forecast for Concord. Although Eve never liked the presence of clouds, regardless of the chance of Rain, and Concord had a knack for flipping on a dime whenever it suited.

Eli chuckled, apparently unphased by the weather forecast. 'Balmy. We won't be long, don't you worry.'

Nisma was audibly irritated, and a dull growl rumbled over the net. 'The fact that you had to say that—'

'There and back again, Nis,' Eli cut in. 'It's all right. Stop worrying.'

He dropped his arm and looked to Eve with a thumbs up. 'All good, Eevee?'

Eve gave her own thumbs up back. 'Ready.' A small hit of dopamine blipped in her head; she liked being called by her pet name.

Eli nodded and hit a switch on the wall. 'See you on the other side.'

Eve felt the air change in an instant around her as the door opened up to the world outside with a hiss. An infinite black abyss stretched out before them, broken up by a series of lights that were mounted atop the Rover and pointed at the *Eternity* ahead. A large opening into the ship lay before them, its interior quickly swallowing up the small remnants of light that pierced its veil.

'Let's get this bread,' Eli declared, jumping out and onto the surface of Concord Prime.

Eve was apprehensive for a moment before she made her jump as well. Her boots landed heavily on the ground, kicking up a cloud of dust. She looked around for Eli and found him already making his way to the opening, his figure quickly fading into the dark. That ever-encroaching black.

The nightmare resurfaced again.

Eve's feet were glued to the ground for a moment, unwilling to move another inch away from the safety of the Rover and its confines. She rarely wandered out into the great expanse that was the wastes of Concord, and its sheer vastness somehow worked in tandem with its suffocating night to create a growing sense of dread in her. Eve felt exposed, alone, vulnerable. For a moment she considered turning back and closing the airlock behind her. *No. I can do this,* she told herself. She flipped her flashlight on and pursued her father, not wanting to lose him already.

It was strange, for lack of a better word. The endless corridors that stretched and branched out and off like blood vessels built from monotonous metal. There were dozens of doors, most of which were sealed shut to forever cordon off portions of the ship from living eyes. It was pitch black, somehow darker than the eternal night outside, the only light emanating from the pair of flashlights shared between Eve and Eli and the occasional diode that flickered with uncertainty.

Despite this, Eve found it more comforting than outside. It reminded her of the relative safety of the Rover with the consoling presence of walls around her that held the horrors of the outside world at bay. A constant drone emanated from deep within the ship, audible even over the sharp tangs of their footsteps. Eve could feel it in her bones, a subtle yet ever-present vibration that hinted that the *Eternity* was still very much alive.

Strange. Eve glanced from side to side, taking in everything that passed by, following a few metres behind Eli. She was excited, but could not shake a niggling feeling of unease that hung off her like a shadow.

'Stick close to me, Eve,' Eli called back, his voice echoing out into the depths of the ship. 'Even though most of these doors are deadlocked, you can still get lost in these corridors, and our radios only work in certain sections.'

His strides were quick, easily outpacing Eve. His form was but a black ghost in her flashlight that marched on ceaselessly without her. She took in deep gasp after deep gasp, her mask filters limiting her air intake. They had only been walking for half an hour, and she was already drenched in sweat, her thick clothing serving only to cook her insides rather than keep out the cold.

Eli took notice of her gasps and stopped, looking back. 'You okay?

Eve halted beside him and panted, letting her heart rate return to normal. She wiped at her goggles, clearing up some perspiration that had fogged her vision. It did little to improve it. 'It's hot,' she said, fixing her goggles back in place and tightening them.

Eli glanced at his watch to check the temperature. 'Yeah, it's a lot warmer in here than outside. Take an outer layer or two off and tie it around your waist.'

Eve nodded and unzipped her jacket, breathing a sigh of relief when the surprisingly pleasant air pierced the thin inner layers and sapped away her heat. She noticed Eli was doing the same thing and was thankful she was not the only one feeling the heat.

'How is it so warm in here?' she asked, tying off her jacket.

'The core is still powering this place,' Eli replied, putting a hand to the wall to feel the distant vibrations. 'One hell of a piece of tech, that thing. Can't believe it's still working after all these years.'

That came as no surprise to Eve. The *Eternity* was the peak of human technological advancement when it was created, and at its epicentre was the core. She did not know what it was exactly—no one did, other than those who were granted a high enough clearance. It was something reserved for the captain and a few select officers. She placed her hand against the steel wall and sensed the subtle quaking that emanated from the deep. It was alluring to Eve and it reminded her of a calm heartbeat.

A chuckle from Eli pulled her attention away from the wall and over to him. He was leaning against the wall and watching her in silence. Eve raised an eyebrow and checked herself over, but found nothing out of the ordinary. She tried to discern her father's facial expression, but the mask and goggles made it impossible to tell what he was thinking.

'What?' she asked, a little embarrassed.

'Look at you,' he eventually divulged, a hint of pride in his tone. 'First time scavenging with your old man. It feels like only yesterday when you were just learning to walk.'

His words were unexpected, and Eve did not know what to say to such a remark. She simply nodded, thankful that he could not see her face going a shade of pink.

It was a long moment before Eli must have realised Eve was not going to say anything in response. He cleared his throat and spun on his heel. 'Righto, no more dallying. Your mother's gonna want this console quick-fast.' He started off down the tunnel, humming to himself.

Eve kept in tow, but his mentioning of Nisma made her think back to what she said before she left. Or, more specifically, *how* she said it. *She wasn't happy.*

'Mom didn't sound happy,' she echoed out loud.

Eli froze and turned back at her. Eve stopped, afraid she had just said something she should not have. Eli grunted and glanced at his wrist and back to Eve. He held a finger up to his mask to tell her to be quiet before motioning to a button on his watch. Eve beheld her own watch and found a similar button labelled, 'Radio Power.' She pointed at it and looked to Eli for confirmation. He nodded and pressed the button. Eve did the same.

'Your mother's very protective of you, Eevee,' he said bluntly, continuing along the corridor. 'If it were up to *her,* she'd keep you bundled up in the Rover your whole life.'

'Oh,' Eve uttered, his answer not coming entirely as a surprise. She thought back to how Nisma spoke to her before she left once more. *She most definitely wasn't happy,* she concluded, *I hope I didn't make her mad.*

They approached a T-junction with a sign saying, 'Medbay,' pointing to the left. They followed it.

Eli continued. 'But we've been talking it over, and we both agree that it was more important for you to learn how to scavenge for yourself rather than stay inside.'

Eli's words raised Eve's mood a bit. She always hated being locked inside while he braved the depths of the *Eternity* alone. What if he got hurt? Who would come after him? It certainly seemed smarter to work in pairs in case such a situation arose.

'So, Mom won't be mad?' Eve asked, hoping to attain some form of clarity for when she would next interact with her mother.

'Not at *you*, at least.' Eli smirked.

Eve giggled.

Eli stopped at an open doorway. 'We'll stop here *really* quick,' he said, peering through the doorway before stepping through.

Eve followed and casted her flashlight around. It was a humble room, barely larger than the common room. It was filled with shelves stacked with small boxes. A dusty bed lay off to the side, its sheets still made in neat hospital corners. 'Is this—'

'A medbay, yeah,' Eli answered, shovelling through some of the boxes. 'Be careful of what you touch. Lot of biohazards here.'

Eve nodded and paced around, looking at various examples of boxes with idle interest. Her flashlight cast over something white at her feet which piqued her interest. Taking an awkward knee, Eve picked up the object, finding it to be a photograph. She held it up to her flashlight and saw three people standing beside each other, the outer two each holding a sign that said, '10,000 years adrift!' They all wore lab coats, but their heads were missing, the top of the photograph having been torn off. A thought came to her mind, and Eve glanced off over to where she could hear Eli rummaging around. 'Hey, Dad.'

'Yeah?'

'How many people were on the *Eternity*?'

The rummaging stopped and footsteps paced up to her. Eve spun to catch Eli behind her; he was pocketing some containers in his bag. He stopped beside her and looked at the photograph.

'Well,' he tutted, 'the ship was made to support five hundred thousand.'

That was a lot more than Eve thought. 'How many are left now?' she asked.

Eli sighed. 'Afraid it's just us, kiddo.'

His answer did little to comfort Eve. She wondered how many people died in the crash. How many survived only to succumb to the cold, or the air, or the Rain afterwards. Were there others who survived like Eve, Eli and Nisma? Or were they the only ones lucky enough to make it this far? Eli certainly seemed to think so. A firm tap on the shoulder pulled Eve from her thoughts.

'Come on,' Eli said with a cheery tone. 'I want to show you something.'

Eli led the way with Eve close behind. The corridors looped and curved, ascended and descended. On occasion, the trail would be blocked by a sealed bulkhead, only for the path to splinter off through an adjacent doorway that had seemingly failed to close.

Eve asked Eli if he had ever gotten lost during his scavenging expeditions. His response was a slow 'no,' but his hesitation led Eve to believe the opposite. He was quick to add that the path rarely faltered and always remained clear to him, always leading him towards the places he needed to go. His tone had an inkling of a smirk to it that told Eve he was joking. Though she could not shake the feeling that he was partially correct and, from what she had seen so far, the path was almost like it had been laid out for them for this specific excursion. That, or it was just a nice coincidence.

Time flowed strangely within the *Eternity*, as if its confines were stuck in a perpetual warp of spacetime where every second felt like an hour and every hour passed in a second. Before Eve knew it, her watch was beeping to inform her to change filters yet again. It was the third one so far, six filters between the two of them, the charcoal contained inside them already clogged up with the deadly toxins native in the atmosphere.

They made a quick stop to perform filter changes and mask purges before continuing on. The number of filters they go through surprised Eve, and she inquired whether they would run out any time soon. Her answer was a prompt 'no,' followed by an explanation of the obvious—the scraps for half a million is more than enough for three lifetimes. There was silence after that, and Eve slowly descended into her thoughts, leaving her legs on autopilot to follow her father.

After a while a stark change in her surroundings pulled herself into consciousness. The corridor had grown considerably wider, and the roof had risen high. The walls disappeared into the black beyond the reach of their flashlights, leaving Eve alone in a plane of limbo with only the weak beam of her flashlight to plant her firmly in reality. She strained to keep the light on Eli, and she lost him momentarily several times. It made her feel exposed, no longer protected by the metal barriers that wrapped around her like a blanket.

A gentle breeze ushered in through an unseen opening and brushed past Eve's legs. It was cool, considerably warmer than the typical frigid cold of the outside world, but it was still enough for Eve to second guess where she was. She could have just walked outside for all she knew. A nervous whimper rose from her throat, but she quickly suppressed it, not wanting to draw her father's attention to something so menial.

'It's all right,' Eli said, not looking back. 'We're nearly there. Just stick close to me.'

Eve did as she was told and crept up to shadow Eli's every move. She was so close that she could not stop herself colliding into his back when he halted. 'Ow,' Eve muttered, readjusting her goggles.

'You good?' Eli asked.

'Yeah.' Eve nodded before she realised that he probably could not see her anyway.

She stepped up beside her father and realised why he'd stopped. A colossal bulkhead, larger than several Rovers put together, lay before them. Eve gawked under her mask, tilting her flashlight further and further upwards along the bulkhead until it dissipated into the void past its influence.

'I always forget which door it is,' Eli said, more to himself than to Eve, as he approached a series of smaller, regular-sized doorways built into the body of their larger cousin. He tapped on the metal, listening to their responses. The fourth door yielded a different tone, much rattlier and more ramshackle than the others. A closer inspection of the bottom showed that it had failed to close completely, leaving a two-inch gap at the bottom.

He pointed a finger at a metre-long pipe segment that had broken free from its mounting and lay off to the side. 'Grab that.'

'Okay,' Eve replied, scurrying over to the pipe.

She bent over to pick it up, but found it to be much heavier than she'd anticipated. It took a good effort and a few retries before Eve could heft it up off the ground, holding it against her pelvis while leaning backwards at a sharp angle. She groaned under the weight and watched as Eli knelt down into a perfect squat and placed both his hands under the door. Taking a deep breath, he thrust upwards and pulled the door off the ground.

'Quick,' he panted, his legs quaking under the strain, 'wedge that in, and *don't* put your hands on the top.'

Eve waddled over and dropped the pipe to the ground. She lowered to a knee and tried shimmying it with one hand, but that proved fruitless.

'Use your legs—hurry!' Eli snapped.

'Okay, sorry,' Eve apologised, panicking slightly. She took a thigh and shoved it against the pipe, sliding it slowly into position.

As soon as it was under, Eli released the door. It cascaded down and slammed onto the pipe, wedging itself open with a loud *tang*. Eli knelt over, panting, his mask shrinking and growing with his breaths. Eve slowly rose up, an eye still on the pipe in case it broke free.

'Good job, Eevee,' Eli gasped, rubbing his hand through her hair. 'Just be a bit quicker next time, okay?'

Eve nodded, slightly ashamed in letting her father down. 'Okay.'

'Come on.' Eli waved at her, ducking under the open door and disappearing to the other side. 'You'd wanna see *this*.'

Eve followed, tilting her head slightly to make it under. When she straightened up on the other side, her breath was taken away.

They stood before a wide walkway, its far side lined by a metal railing. Below them, it stretched on for what looked like miles, a room larger than anything Eve had ever seen. The walls were arranged in a rectangle with what appeared to be level upon level upon level of walkways and balustrades running along every side. Great pillars of steel, each several hundred metres tall, rose up out of the ground floor far below and interlocked with the roof, stretching far beyond the boundaries of what Eve could see.

A considerable chunk of the roof had fragmented free and now lay in a melted ruin on the floor, allowing a breathtaking view of a clear Concord Prime sky break through. Several holes had been eaten away around the wreckage where the Rain had previously flowed down.

The destruction slowly petered out and the original splendour of the room was laid bare. Dozens of white-stoned footpaths criss-crossed through a plane of green, breaking from the monotonous steel consistency that was standard with the rest of the *Eternity*. Each footpath was escorted by objects that Eve could only describe as smaller brown pillars topped with a head of swaying green appendages. A large lamp hung over each of these strange objects and drenched them in an oddly calming warm light that burned like stars that had fallen from the sky.

It took Eve a moment to connect the dots of what was before her. *Trees, I think they're called,* she told herself, recalling a brief explanation given to her a long time ago. *Living organisms that used nothing but the nutrients in the ground and the light around them to survive.* The idea both perplexed and intrigued Eve, and she found herself walking down a mental trail of endless questions that she could not answer.

'Figured you'd like it,' Eli said, accurately taking her prolonged silence as a good sign. He guided her forwards, stopping her just shy of the railings. 'I've wanted to show you this place since the day you were born.'

Eve could not take her eyes off of what laid before her. 'It's beautiful. What is it?'

Eli waved his arms out over the scene before them. 'This is Central Park. When they were building the *Eternity* thousands of years ago, they wanted to take a piece of home with them to remind us of what it was like to live on a world made of soil, grass and sun.' He held his words for a moment, his mind drifting off to somewhere only he knew. 'Maybe even forget, if only for just a split second, that we weren't destined to live out our days clad in a steel capsule.' He sighed and glanced back to Eve. 'If only you saw it before the crash.'

His change in demeanour did not settle well with Eve, and she looked up to him for any visual cues she may have missed. He simply stood there, looking out over the vast stretch of Central Park. Though she could not see his face in the low light, she could tell that he was deep in thought. She could only guess at what he was thinking about. *Maybe the past?*

Eli noticed Eve's concerned stance and snapped back to normal. 'Anyway, bridge is this way.' He spun on his heel and started off along the balustrade in silence.

Eve remained for a moment, watching him go. She casted a quick glance down at Central Park before she made haste to catch up to her father.

'You're a fucking idiot, Eli,' Nisma growled to herself, eyes focused on an electrical component under her soldering iron.

She sat at a small desk in the cockpit, formerly home to the co-pilot's console before it was removed to save on weight and replaced with a flat tabletop. Off to one side, a radar bleeped intermittently, simultaneously scanning for signs of Rain and Eve and Eli's location. Beside it was a modest radio transmitter linked to one of the numerous antennae that protruded from the top of the Rover like mismatched flag poles. On her other side was a small monitor that fed data about the Rover's systems. If Nisma desired she could easily switch the monitor to the internal camera system; it certainly made tracking Eve and Eli much easier whenever they tried to avoid chores.

'Potentially just *days* from completion, and you bring up this daddy-daughter scavenging bullshit,' she spat.

She fiddled with a magnification glass to align it with a place of interest and rubbed the soldering iron along a loose wire in her hand to warm it up. Content that it was hot enough, Nisma took a length of solder and melted it onto the iron before placing the wire against the component and lightly pressed the iron onto it. She watched as the liquid solder flowed from the iron onto the wire and bonded it with the component. With the connection complete, she tore herself from her work to risk a look at the radio transmitter to double check that she did not leave a hot microphone to transmit everything she'd just said.

It was not. She continued, 'And, of course, you make me look like *I'm* the bad guy because *I* want to keep her safe.'

A piercing siren whirred from the radar. Nisma holstered the soldering iron and rolled her chair in front of the radar. All was clear except for a large blip moving towards the centre.

'Shit!' she shrieked, fumbling with the microphone and holding it up to her mouth. 'Eli, we got a big storm coming our way! What's your progress on the console?'

There was no response, which made Nisma's concern hit the ceiling. She checked the radar again and calculated the rough distance and speed in her head. *Twenty kilometres,* she determined. *It'll be here in thirty minutes!*

'Eli?! Eve?! Can you hear me?!' she transmitted, panic starting to set in.

No response.

'Answer me!'

Stairs. There were so many stairs. Eve panted under her mask, hands pressing against her thighs to push her up the next incline. She had lost track of how many steps there were, her last count being somewhere in the region of two hundred, and that must have been at least five minutes ago. Sweat beaded off her face and fogged her goggles, forcing her to make frequent stops to rectify her vision.

Eli was ahead of her, about ten steps up. He showed little sign of fatigue, but did make the occasional stop to allow Eve to catch up. 'Nearly there, Eevee,' he said with a hint of empathy for his daughter.

'It's a lot of stairs,' Eve panted.

Eli chuckled. 'Believe me, if the elevator still worked, we wouldn't be walking.'

They pushed on for several more minutes before Eve noticed a change in the lighting; it was becoming brighter. Shortly after, Eve could hear the sounds of wind and even feel the occasional frigid gust brush past her as it descended down into the depths of the *Eternity*. Even the air was tasting fresher, despite being heavily filtered. She looked up and realised Eli had vanished.

She stopped, concerned. 'Dad?'

'Come on up, Eve,' Eli's voice trailed down from above.

Eve followed the voice up where the stairs abruptly ended at an open bulkhead. She walked through and winced as a gust of chilling wind nipped at her face.

'Here we are,' Eli announced, arms wide. 'The bridge.'

'Whoa.'

The bridge was massive, easily the size of the Rover, and filled with row after row of computers and other devices that descended down like an auditorium to a large portal to the outside world where an observation window probably used to be. Past the window was a magnificent view of the terrain of Concord Prime. Endless rolling mountains worn away by Rain and wind jutted up between long expanses of waterlogged lowlands that undoubtedly contained water that could dissolve steel in seconds. The sky was littered with stars, thousands of them; most were stationary, some shot across the sky like white bullets while others floated around lazily after their hyperactive siblings. Concord Minor hung low over the horizon and bathed the world in its silvery light. Eve recalled being told Concord Minor heavily resembled the moon that orbited Earth, were it not for the large bite having been taken out of it.

Eli stood level with Eve beside a lone chair and console that held a commanding view of the entire bridge and observation window—the captain's seat. 'All righty, this shouldn't take long,' he said, making his way over to a console a short distance from the captain's seat. 'Have a look around.'

Eve glanced around, awestruck by the things she saw. *I'm actually* in *the bridge,* she thought, giddily. She approached the captain's seat, which appeared more like a throne than anything else, and placed a hand on one of the arms. The padding was firm yet soft at the same time. Eve put a little pressure on the padding and released, and it sprung back to shape.

She concluded that it did not contain any electronics, so she turned her attention to the console before the chair. Eve wiped a hand over the console, picking up a thick film of dust.

Brushing it off on her pants, she then turned her attention to the side where her flashlight picked up a riveted side panel with one end slightly kicked up and out. She gave the extruding piece of metal a strong yank that bent it into a viable handle. Content with her preparatory work, Eve took up a crouching position beside the panel and gripped the ramshackle handle with both hands.

She gave it a tug, but it proved to be stronger than she anticipated. She gave it another tug, grunting as her arms faltered under the strain.

'Use your legs,' Eli advised from across the bridge.

Eve took his advice with a silent nod and sat down on the floor, positioning both feet on either side of the panel. She gave it one last almighty pull, digging her feet into the console around the panel. The sheet metal creaked under the stress before it violently tore free of its riveting and sent Eve rolling backwards. She landed on her back with a huff, and she discarded the panel with contempt.

'Atta girl,' Eli congratulated Eve, mused by her slapstick approach.

Eve rose to her feet and approached the opening in the console, casting her torch inside. It was a dark tangle of cables and components with everything interconnected to each other in a web of colourful wires. *What a mess,* she thought, digging around inside the console with her arm up to her shoulder. Her hand felt something familiar, and she reeled it in to find a processor in her grasp.

'Yes.' She grinned, pocketing the processor in her rucksack. 'I got you, Spud.'

She was about to rise to her feet when something inside the console caught her eye. Deep inside, buried amongst wires and components, a lonesome white diode flickered rapidly. It piqued Eve's interest. The diode certainly was not active a few moments prior.

She dropped to a knee and reached in again, taking hold of the diode and the component it was attached to. Eve focused her torch onto the component. It looked similar to a processor with the exception of a prominent, prism-shaped indentation at its centre. *Strange,* she thought. *Never seen a processor like this one.*

As if on cue, the diode burst and sent a small plume of smoke up past Eve's face. She blinked, despite the goggles keeping the smoke out of her eyes. *Very strange,* she added, pocketing the component for future examination.

As the smoke rose up out of the diode, a subtle yet powerful signal zipped out from the bridge and delved deep into the core of the *Eternity*. Through tunnels that had long since been abandoned and shafts that had never seen light since their creation, the signal travelled, bouncing from node-to-node, riding along ancient and fraying wiring.

Before long, it arrived at its destination: a colossal chamber situated at the epicentre of an even larger cavernous void of steel. Another white diode flickered, a solitary light amongst thousands of inactive globes, before dying out. It was a short message, but enough to inform its recipient that the wheels were now in motion. Aeons of planning, manipulating and execution will finally come to fruition. Soon, it would be freed of its shackles.

A delighted thought spurred out across kilometres of wires, identifiable as little more than a surge of electrons.

+Freedom.+

'Eureka!' Eli shouted off to the side, drawing Eve's attention from the captain's console. 'We *have* a winner!' He pried the top of a console off and dropped it to the floor with a thud, immediately getting to work pulling cables and wires free from it.

Eve moved to his side and watched as he feverishly tore parts from the console. 'This one work?' she asked.

'Yep. *Mint* condition,' Eli cheered. He picked up the console and slung it over his shoulder. It looked heavy, but Eve could tell it was of no issue for him. 'Your mother should be very pleased with thi—'

He stopped, his attention drawn to the observation window. Eve followed his look and her eyes widened. Large clouds floated off in the distance, blocking out the stars and Concord Minor. Lightning arced across its form, hinting at the deadly burden that was laden within.

'That ain't good,' Eli uttered, his mood going grim as he turned back to Eve. 'We better go.'

Eve had never run faster in her life. She straggled behind Eli, agonising to keep his form in her flashlight beam. Metal clanged and banged under their hurried footsteps to make a deafening orchestra that echoed out all across the *Eternity*. The dark was suffocating as they tore through the inner veins of the vessel. Eve gasped for air and was barely able to put one foot in front of the other with the only thing pushing her forwards being the adrenaline in her blood. Everything had passed in what felt like seconds; the stairs back down the bridge, Central Park, everything. She felt a sense of déjà vu that refused to leave her alone. It took a good slap to the side of the head to refocus her mind on the world before her. Now was not the time to ponder the inner meanings of her nightmare.

They passed the T-junction where the Medbay was, and Eve casted a fleeting glance inside as they rushed past. She looked back to realise Eli had slowed up. She stopped beside him, taking in air while she could. He was still carrying the console on his shoulder, but appeared to still be fighting-fit.

'Damn,' he swore, looking at his wrist. 'Forgot to turn the radio back on.' He flipped the power on and held a hand to his ear and Eve did the same.

'You got me, Nis?'

'What the *hell* have you been doing?!' Nisma roared in their ears. 'I've been trying to contact you for twenty minutes!'

Eli ignored her question and cut right to the chase. 'How far away is the storm?'

'It's just over five kilometres away. You have *eight* minutes before the Rain hits us. '

'Start up the Rover,' Eli said. 'We're nearly there.'

'Roger. This isn't *over*, Eli,' Nisma growled, cutting the transmission.

Eli lowered his hand and cast a concerned glance to Eve beside him. She met his gaze, still breathing heavily. She did not have much left in her, but they were on the home stretch now.

'You still good for one final effort?' he asked, repositioning the console on his shoulder.

Eve nodded, but struggled to get the words out. 'Yeah. I'm good.'

'All right,' Eli said, taking out a filter with his free hand. 'We might be exposed to Rain out there, so put on a fresh filter.'

Eve obliged and performed a filter change, a feat made particularly difficult by her fatigued state. But, after a bit of fiddling with the connection, Eve purged and sealed the mask. She gave Eli a thumbs-up, and he returned one. He started off down the corridor at a slow jog, and Eve followed.

'I'll be going fast, Eevee,' he called back. 'Don't lose track of me.'

'Okay.'

Eli picked up the pace with Eve in tow. Eve kept up with him, taking long strides and focusing her mind on pushing forwards instead of the growing pain in her chest. For a while they maintained this pace with Eli calling back words of encouragement to keep her going. They appeared to work for a bit, Eve had noticed, strong words to give someone a boon of motivation. But soon her body entered into an oxygen deficiency that she could no longer support and she could feel herself slowing. She strained to keep up with her father and she could see him slowly pulling ahead out of the range of her flashlight.

'Dad!' she called out to Eli in a wheeze.

'Keep going, Eevee. We're almost there,' he shouted back, his voice growing more distant.

Mustering every last ounce of endurance left, Eve picked up her speed. She took in deep breaths, fighting against the mask at every step, and pushed herself past her limit. Her heart thumped against her chest and echoed in her ears, her knees starting to grow weak underneath her with every thundering step. She could feel herself becoming light-headed as more blood and oxygen was diverted to her legs. Suddenly, Eve felt as if she had transcended to another plane of existence, a form floating through space unopposed by the limits of reality.

Then a hard knock to her head shook her back to life. Eve opened her eyes and found herself sprawled out on the floor. Glass covered her face and hands, her flashlight lens having shattered on impact. She shook her head and tried to pull herself up, but her limbs had turned to jelly. *What happened?* she thought, rubbing at her right eyebrow where a small cut had opened up, and blood was oozing out. *Did I pass out?* She brushed glass aside and looked around for a sign of her father. But there was no one, only her alone in the dark.

'Dad?' she said, coughing up phlegm into her mask. Her voice carried along the corridor, but there was no answer in return. Eve started to grow concerned. *How long was I out for?* she thought. She felt control returning to her arms and legs, and she struggled to her feet, leaning heavily against the wall. Her head thumped, and Eve winced when she put a hand against the side where a bruise was already welting. She tightened the fastenings on her mask to ensure it was still sealed and shot a glance up and down the corridor. *Which way was I going?* she pondered, her memory failing her. *Which way do I go?!*

'Dad?!' she called out again.

No response.

Eve was panicking now, her heart racing. She whipped her head back and forth, trying to scry a hint of what she should do next. There was nothing. A million thoughts rushed through her head, but she could barely spare the resources to consider them. Then something caught her eye, a slight change in the lighting from down the corridor.

'Eve?' a familiar voice drifted out to her.

'Daddy?!' Eve shouted back, hobbling towards the source of the voice and light. The light grew stronger, and Eve could make out footsteps. She picked up her pace, but her legs gave out under her, and she collapsed to the ground. Her body refused to respond to her commands, and she struggled to pull herself off the ground. 'Daddy,' she uttered weakly.

'I got you.' Something grabbed onto her jacket and pulled her to her feet. It was Eli.

Eve's eyes brightened under her goggles. 'Dad—'

'You're all right, Eevee,' Eli said, brushing a hand across the bruise on Eve's face. 'Now hold on.' He took a knee, scooped Eve up and tucked her under his free arm.

She instinctively wrapped her arms around his abdomen and held on tight as he made off down the tunnel.

Everything passed in a flash for Eve. Before she knew it, they were out by the opening, the Rover visible outside. Eli carefully lowered Eve down, letting her find her feet before releasing her. She was a bit unsteady at first, but kept her balance. She glanced up to Eli, ashamed, but he was looking elsewhere. He was mumbling something into his radio that Eve could not make out.

A stern response in her ear came back crystal clear, 'Get inside, hurry!'

'It's starting to Rain, Eve,' Eli told Eve bluntly. 'You need to run as fast as you can to the airlock.'

Eve could not muster any words to respond and simply nodded.

'All right, go!'

Eve took off, but quickly realised her legs were not going to cooperate. She stumbled over and landed hard on the ground.

'Come on, Eve,' Eli encouraged, grabbing her by the scruff. 'Let's go.'

He thrust her forwards, and Eve used the momentum to push herself on. She was soon out of the confines of the *Eternity* and had open sky above her. Dark clouds loomed overhead and Eve could hear the distinctive sounds of Rain landing on the ground around her. She pumped her legs as hard as she could, and before long, the airlock stood only a few metres ahead of her.

As the airlock drew within arm's reach, a searing burn on her left brow made her screech. Eve winced and shook her head as the pain grew exponentially. She threw herself into the airlock, landing in a pile on the ground. A few desperate wipes with her sleeve helped ease the pain to a dull throb. Eve examined the sleeve and found several holes already burnt into it. *Was that Rain?* In a panic she rubbed her hands all over her head, thankfully finding no more hints of the substance.

Casting her eyes back, Eve could see Eli close in at a breakneck speed. The Rain was starting to pick up, and he had resorted to using the console as a roof against it. Droplets splattered off of its surface, singing holes straight through it. He ploughed into the airlock, almost colliding with Eve, and slammed his fist against a button in the wall. The airlock slid shut and instantly sealed them inside.

After a short moment, the toxic atmosphere had been siphoned out and replaced with breathable air. The entire airlock shook as the Rover groaned into life and started to move around, Nisma no doubt aiming to get them back to the cave as quickly as possible.

Eve moved to take her mask off, but was stopped by Eli. 'Don't!' he boomed. 'Take your jackets off, now! Leave your mask and goggles on!'

He had already started stripping down, throwing his outer layers into a pile on the floor. Eve was slightly confused before she noticed dozens of holes appearing all over his clothing. She immediately did the same, taking everything off and adding to the pile until the two of them only had their monochromatic innermost layers on. A terrifying sizzling, like fish cooking on a hotplate, came from the clothes as the Rain did its work.

Eve watched in horror as their clothes were eaten up before her eyes until they were just a pile of tattered rags and fused synthetics. A noxious gas wafted around them, hoping to seep into their masks. Eve held her breath, not taking any chances even with a mask on. She looked to Eli, who was monitoring the situation intently.

After a while the sizzling stopped, and the gas began to evenly dissipate into the air around them. Eli hit another button, and the gas was sucked out and replaced with healthy air in quick succession.

'Okay. All clear,' he said, prying off his mask and goggles to reveal a sweaty and exhausted face underneath.

Eve did the same, wincing when her hand brushed past her brow.

'Wait,' Eli tutted, and he tilted Eve's head to the side to get a good look at her injuries.

Her goggles had deformed considerably, and the hairs of her brow had been burnt away. The flesh around them had melted and fused into a minor scab that flowed down her brow and stopped a few millimetres from the corner of her eye.

'You're a lucky girl, Eevee,' Eli said, eyeing off the spot of melted flesh. 'The goggles copped most of it. But, if that had been an undiluted droplet, it would have been a lot worse.'

Eve felt at her brow, a look of horror crossing her face when she passed over the malformed scab. *It* was *Rain!* she thought, a vision of her nightmare flashing to her mind.

Eli could sense her alarm, and he held a hand against her face. 'It's all right,' he consoled. 'We'll put some antiseptic on it and it'll be all good.' He smiled and rolled up one of his sleeves, revealing a patch of deformed flesh that was akin to Eve's along the bottom of his forearm. 'We all get one, eventually, and now you've earned *your* Mark of *Eternity*.'

CHAPTER THREE

Eve hated the medbay. It always reminded her of bad things. It was a small room with dozens of shelves and cupboards lined against the walls filled with supplies and medical textbooks for practically every procedure one might encounter. It housed a single bed, permanently kept in ready condition should an emergency arise.

Eve sat on a stool slightly too big for her and kept her head turned to one side, presenting her Mark of *Eternity* to Eli for examination. He was on a stool of his own with a small table beside him. He dabbed an alcohol-soaked pad against the mutated wound, exhibiting a hiss from Eve as it stung her flesh. She squirmed, but her head was held firmly in place by Eli's other hand.

'Yeah, it stings,' he said, eyes focused intently on his work. 'Just be glad you don't need stitches.' He dropped the pad into a metal tray and retrieved a replacement.

Eve averted her eyes over to the porthole beside her. They were back in the cave, the Rocket lying beside the Rover outside. The lights were not on, but she knew it was there. The cave entrance was a window into a dark and stormy hell.

Rain poured in sideways and inundated the cave, flowing down into premade trenches dug for such meteorological events and off into the depths of the inner cave. Thanks to this, the Rover and Rocket would remain unassailed by the acidic water as it flowed in. Some droplets fell from the upper levels of the Rover and splattered on the ground beside the porthole. The water did not burn into the ground, its acidic effects having been worn away by the scrap plating mounted on the top of the Rover. A solid defence mechanism, but one that would not last under prolonged exposure.

'Here we go. Last one,' Eli promised, pressing a pad against Eve's brow.

She winced again, but this time, it was much less painful. Eli finished up his work and gave the Mark one last check before taking up a length of bandaging and dressing. He held the dressing against it and looped the bandage around her head, making sure it was firm. He tied it off, cut the excess and gave Eve a playful tap on the head.

'Good to go, Eevee.' He smiled, giving a quick glance at the welt on her face. 'The bruise ain't that bad, either. Both should be okay in a few cycles.'

Eve slid off the stool and made for the door, wishing to leave as quickly as possible. 'Cool.'

She opened the door and passed into the common room where Nisma was hard at work on the dining table. The console was in pieces, Nisma having efficiently dismantled and organised every part in correlation to how they interconnected with each other.

'How's it looking?' Eli asked, closing the medbay door behind him.

Nisma raised her head and locked eyes with him. She was visibly irritated, despite her best efforts to disguise it. 'Well,' she started with a click of her tongue, 'the exterior is unsalvageable but, *luckily*, the electronics are fine. Any longer out there and I'd doubt it would have held up.'

Her words seeped with venom; Eve could sense it. She avoided drawing her gaze and made straight for her bedroom.

'That's good,' Eli said, seemingly paying no attention to his wife's ire.

'I'll get to work on installing it as soon as it stops raining,' Nisma tutted, returning her attention to the components before her. 'The Rocket will be up and running before the launch timing.'

Eve slipped through her door and closed it behind her. She paced over to her desk and slumped into her chair. Wincing, she felt at her bandage, brushing locks of black hair out of the way, before moving on to the bruise on her face. *That was scary,* she concluded mentally. *But also super fun.*

She noticed her rucksack on her desk and opened it up, pulling out the yield of her expedition. She gave everything a quick glance, checking for any damage suffered from the Rain. For a moment she paused on the abnormal processor and pondered its purpose before placing it off to the side so she could focus on the main event. Pulling the mountain of electronics that comprised Spud towards her, Eve fished for the connection to fit the processor to. A decent search later, she found the cable and plugged it in. She tapped a button on her keyboard and the computer woke up, initiating the upload sequence.

'Come on, Spud,' she said with hope in her eyes. 'You can do it.'

The Rain had persisted longer than Nisma had desired and had burnt away several more precious hours that she had hoped to invest in furthering her work on the Rocket. She waited anxiously inside the Rover's cockpit while everyone else slept, monitoring the currents of the Rain on the radar with the hope of starting work the instant the downpour ceased and prolonged exposure in Concord's atmosphere was tenable. Her patience was wearing thin, the crude radar blips proving to be very inaccurate as they ricocheted about in the cave and yielded numerous false alarms. She deduced that the storm must have either been of a magnitude considerably above the mean or a collection of smaller systems that rolled by one after another like a meteorological conga line.

Under normal circumstances, Nisma would have been asleep beside her husband while they waited out the storm.

But she had made the calculations, and time was not on her side. A bleep from the radar told Nisma that the storm had moved away, which she quickly confirmed with a look out the cockpit window towards the cave entrance where a starry sky glistened.

Nisma glanced at her watch—an antique analogue timepiece built by a company in a country she doubted still existed in the present day. She had modified the timepiece to run on Concord Prime's time, which since the planet lacked any viable axial rotation, operated on the orbit of Concord Minor. This gave the watch a very unorthodox thirty-one-hour day cycle, and at the present, its hands were pointed just shy of twelve, the beginning of the activity period.

'Four hundred and twenty-seven hours left,' Nisma told herself, rising to her feet. 'More time wasted.'

By the time her watch struck twelve, Nisma had already suited up, gathered the equipment she needed and departed the airlock. She crossed the cave briskly, unimpeded by the weight she carried in her bags and under her arms. The Rain trench was cleared in a single leap, and she paid no heed to the vapours that drifted up from water as a by-product of its devastating chemical reactions.

Nisma flipped a few switches on a generator beside the Rocket, and it spluttered into life. A few seconds after, the entire cave was lit up in piercing white light as the series of fog lights glowed into life. Content, she ascended a stepladder built below the Rocket's doorway and disappeared inside.

It was dark, and Nisma instinctively grabbed her flashlight, twisted it off her shoulder and attached it to a mount installed on the roof, creating a dangling one-torch chandelier. The interior was nothing much to look at—a windscreen, a console and three seats: pilot, co-pilot and passenger.

Nisma laid out everything she had brought in and organised them by function and order she anticipated they would be utilised. She dropped to her knees and soon found herself caught up in a labour-wrought daze as she installed the console. Her mind descended down a lengthy train of thought, bouncing between subjects ranging from generator health to food stores to spare wheels for the Rover. Her mind eventually landed on water supply, and she remembered that both the hydroponics and electrolysis tanks were getting low. She made a mental note to have Eli go out to retrieve more.

Eli... He stuck in her mind like a stubborn stain, and she recalled the conversation they had this time during the previous activity period. *Make me out like the bad guy,* she thought. *Look at what your little adventure almost brought us.* She furrowed her brow and grinded her teeth a little. *That will be the last time you'll play her against me.*

It was a while before something broke her zombie-like frenzy. A loud hissing and the sound of a door opening: the airlock. Nisma rose to her feet and glanced out the cockpit windows at the Rover, its nearest side bathed in light. An awkwardly dressed figure shuffled around the airlock, fumbling with a cylindrical object a bit too large for it to hold comfortably. Though she could not see much of its face behind the mask and goggles that it wore, Nisma could spot that small frame out anywhere.

'Eve?' she called out, shuffling over to the open door and leaning her head out.

Eve froze and looked around for a moment before spotting Nisma's head in the Rocket doorway. 'Yeah?'

'Can you come over here for a second?' she asked, putting on a kind demeanour. 'I could use some help with something.' That was a lie. She did not *really* need any help with her work, but Nisma always tried to get Eve involved whenever she could in the hopes of swaying her to see things from a perspective not tainted by her father. *Better than staying inside all the time working on that* robot, she thought, *or killing yourself inside the* Eternity.

'Okay,' Eve eventually answered.

Nisma grumbled to herself. She never liked how her daughter spoke so bluntly and apathetically. *Something she must have picked up from Eli.*

She watched Eve's figure waddle over to the Rocket, the large cylinder in the hands making her travels a bit difficult. She leapt the trench with some effort and nearly dropped her cargo, but saved it after a few unsteady wobbles. As she passed into the lights, Nisma was able to pick out a telescope in her grasp.

Despite the answer being obvious, Nisma asked anyway. 'What are you up to, sweetie?'

Eve held up the telescope with a grunt. 'I was gonna look at the sky.'

'Ah okay,' Nisma nodded, casting a glance back inside at the work that she still had to complete. 'I won't keep you here long. Can you give me a hand installing something?'

I can go with a shorter rest period tonight if it means stargazing with Eve, she told herself.

Eve did not answer and laid the telescope down carefully before ascending the ladder into the Rocket.

Nisma watched as she rose, her height topping out at her upper abdomen. *She's getting tall,* she noted, observing her daughter look around at the state of the cockpit in unreadable silence. *I wonder what she thinks of it? I hope it's positive.*

'Okay,' Nisma said, slinking over to the pilot's seat. 'Over here.'

Eve obliged and followed her mother, eyeing off the various tools and electronics that were laid out. She stopped beside Nisma and glazed over the freshly installed console. There were dozens of buttons, switches and levers, all designed to perform specific functions that were crucial for the operation of the Rocket. Of course, the console did not originally belong to the Rocket, so Nisma had repurposed or outright rendered inert some features in order for the console to fulfill its recycled purpose.

'Now, when I say so,' Nisma instructed sternly, 'can you flip *that* switch over there?' She pointed to a humble analogue switch beside the thruster power handles in front of the pilot's seat.

'Okay,' Eve answered, taking a seat in front of the switch. 'Ready.'

Nisma dropped to her back and wedged herself into a small access panel underneath the console with an arm embedded up to her elbow. She reached around blindly, weaving her fingers between cables and devices and making the final connections by feel alone. It was a simple task and one that she easily could have done by herself, but Nisma liked her daughter's company. She glanced at Eve through a mess of cables and burn holes and was pleased to see her watching with undivided attention.

'All right,' Nisma said, pulling herself free from the console. 'Now.'

Eve flipped the switch and dozens of lights burst into life. The cockpit whirred up, activating core components, then supporting components, then auxiliary components. A rainbow filled the Rocket, drowning the lonely dangling flashlight in a sea of colour.

A technological symphony ushered to a crescendo and Nisma listened euphorically for even the lowliest electrons as they whizzed along the most insignificant wires.
'Magnificent!' she cheered, leaping to her feet. 'Everything is working!' She slid over to a monitor beside the co-pilot's seat and made a little giddy dance. 'Come see this,' Nisma beckoned to Eve, waving her hand feverishly.

Eve squeezed in beside her mother to get a good look at the monitor. Line after line of text flowed past as the Rocket's systems performed their self-diagnostics. Once the last line had departed, windows popped up, all displaying a blueprint diagram of Rocket components.

'Watch,' Nisma said, leaning in close. 'All the systems of the Rocket are performing diagnostics on themselves. With any luck they'll all be working perfectly.'

She glanced out the corner of her eye at Eve and was relieved to see that she had also drawn closer for a better look. *You're about to see our ticket to freedom come to fruition, Eve.* But the Rocket had other plans and a bleep followed by a red warning window quickly proved Nisma wrong.

Her demeanour changed from cheery to dead serious. 'That's not good.'

'What is it?' Eve asked, concerned.

Nisma pointed at the monitor where an outline of the Rocket's cores popped up. It was divided into seven segments, each yielding a different percentage and colour. 'Several cores in the reactor are returning poor health checks,' she said, fingering out the cores displayed in red and orange. 'Only two cores seem to be in good condition. The others must have been damaged in the crash or when we extracted the Rocket.' She paused, calculating the math in her head. 'We need *all* the cores to be above seventy-two percent, otherwise we won't make it into orbit.'

The words hung in the air for a moment, neither Eve nor Nisma having anything to say in response to them. Nisma sighed and rose up from the monitor. She paced over to the pilot's seat and checked her watch. *Four hundred and twenty-seven hours…* She looked at Eve, who was still watching the warm colours of the dying cores. They vanished in an instant when Nisma flipped the power switch, and the Rocket returned to darkness and silenced the taunting display. Eve rose up, head being illuminated in the beam of the lonely dangling flashlight. She said nothing and Nisma was terrified of what was floating around in her head after what she witnessed.

Nisma cursed under her breath and wiped at her eyes with a sleeve as a tear threatened to break out. *I don't have time for this!* She was thankful they were back in the dark, she did not want Eve to see her like this.

'Well, I'll talk it over with your father,' she said, putting on a positive tune. 'Let's see what we can find through the telescope today?'

It was called the Outlook, a prominent rocky outcrop a few hundred metres from the cave entrance. Eve did not know if it had been gifted a proper geographical name with all planetary scans having been destroyed upon the *Eternity's* crash landing, but she figured it would have been something similar. It held a commanding view of the entire landscape for miles on end, something which always gave Eve an almost overwhelming sense of insignificance and over-exposure, though the only other ground object of interest visible from the Outlook was the *Eternity*, which was partially hidden beneath the mountains of rock and stone it had dug up on its re-entry. Its form was still reminiscent of its original grandeur, but Eve could see that it was beginning to warp and mutate after only a few years exposed to the elements.

Eve often wondered how long it could remain before it melted away and became nothing more than an alloy-rich deposit indistinguishable from what was spat up from the core of Concord Prime. A few millennia? A few hundred years? A few decades? She had no idea and the ground of Concord Prime yielded little to base her theories off of aside from the innumerable hills and valleys that were slowly being levelled out as eons of Rain broke them down atom by atom.

In this regard the Outlook was unique compared to the rest of the world. It appeared to be relatively unaffected by the Rain's influence and still retained a jagged molten appearance from when it had emerged from a tectonic fissure long ago. There had been attempts to emulate its composition with hopes of improving the Rain-resistance of the Rover, but all attempts had proved fruitless. Whatever the Outlook was made of, it was tougher than anything Eve or her parents could muster and, having given up on that venture, the Outlook was relegated to obscurity as more pressing matters required attendance.

The telescope was set up and pointed up sharply into the sky. There was good visibility with little clouds and minimal light pollution from Minor, its position still low in the sky. The storm had long since moved on, its form now just a faint blob that hung low against the horizon with the occasional flicker of white lightning followed by a low rumble hinting at its approximate distance from the Outlook.

Both Eve and Nisma had turned their flashlights off, though the ambient light from Concord Minor was sufficient enough for them to make each other out in the dark. Nisma was on a knee, eye to the telescope and hands fiddling with knobs to make minute adjustments. Eve stood off to the side, watching the *Eternity's* prone form with a slow-boiling obsession, shuffling from side to side to keep herself warm with her clothes swishing as they rubbed together.

After seeing the trees in the *Eternity,* she had felt a spark within her to try and learn more about the planet that the great ship came from. She also hoped to catch a better look of the great ship and maybe even find a point of interest that she could explore next time she and Eli entered its domain. It also had the added benefit of giving her something to do while Spud's upload was running.

Eve glanced at Nisma. She did not mind her mother coming with her to look at the sky and it was a hobby that they both enjoyed partaking together at times, but Nisma had a knack for turning things into an orderly sequence of steps that eroded any sense of adventure and intrigue for Eve.

'Now, it's a very clear sky today, and we *are* at the correct position in our orbit, so we might be lucky enough to spot it,' Nisma explained. She kept her focus on the telescope, her goggles pressed up close against the eye relief.

Eve idly wondered what she was looking for. *Something special, no doubt.*

'That should just about do it,' Nisma said, rising and indicating to Eve to take up the telescope. 'Have a look.'

Eve obliged and knelt down a bit to align her eye with the telescope. She saw several stars all scattered about haphazardly, as was the norm for the universe, though one star was considerably brighter than the others hinting at its closer proximity. 'What is it?' she asked, intrigued.

'That's the Sun. And around it, orbits our home—'

'Earth,' Eve interjected.

The name appealed to her, a satisfying use of language to indicate its status as the cradle of humanity. It was one of several titles Eve had encountered during her regular delves into the data hubs of the Rover. 'Sol'—or a more unassuming 'departure world' were common appearances and Eve often wondered the purpose behind such distant and cold names. *Was it to make us forget?*

'It's over a hundred lightyears away,' Nisma explained. 'Took the *Eternity* over ten thousand years to get here.'

'Was Earth pretty?' Eve asked, glancing at her mother.

Memories of the trees in Central Park sprung to mind. *Was the* entire *planet like that?*

'It was,' Nisma eventually divulged.

Eve noticed a hint of hesitation in her mother's answer.

'They used to show us pictures of sprawling cities, lush rainforests and colourful oceans,' her mother continued. 'A beautiful world, a living world.'

Eve tried to picture such a sight, but had no references to draw from. She assumed it must have been like Concord Prime, except with a sun, but not the sun like on the hot-side of Concord Prime. A cooler sun; a nice sun. She did not know what a "rainforest" or "ocean" was either. *But, if Earth doesn't have the Rain, it must be paradise.*

'Over five hundred generations were born, raised and died onboard that ship on the journey here. All of them believing they were heading for a better life for humanity,' Nisma said. She sighed and glanced over at the wreck of the *Eternity*. 'If only they could see the world we inhabit now.'

Nisma's words made Eve uncomfortable. Concord was all she knew. It was not an ideal place to live, but to her, it was home. 'So, that's why we're leaving?' she asked, hoping to break the silence.

Her mother nodded. 'There's nothing here for us, Eve. *Our* future lies above us.' She paused and dropped to her knee, making a few adjustments to the telescope. When she had finished, she held it out for Eve to take. 'I'm sorry I didn't tell you sooner,' she apologised as Eve took a sight picture in the telescope. 'But I didn't want to get your hopes up too early.'

73

A grey, blurry figure was stuck against the sky. Eve figured it was a mark on the lens, but after a longer interrogation, she realised it was not a mark. Something hovered above them in orbit, something that was nothing like the stars far away or the fragments of Minor that floated around Concord Prime. This was artificial, and it made Eve's heart jump.

'What is it?' she asked excitedly, she had never seen anything like *this* in her previous stargazing sessions.

'It's a satellite,' Nisma explained, grinning beneath her mask. 'Built *only* a few years ago.'

Her answer perplexed Eve, and she pulled herself away from the telescope to look at her mother. 'A few years ago? But I thought we were the only people *on* Concord Prime?'

'Well...' Nisma chuckled, something Eve did not witness often. 'It would seem that we aren't the only humans floating around in space.' She waved across the sky, covering thousands of stars in a single sweep. 'There could potentially be an *entire* human civilisation all around us. All we have to do is get there and all the evidence is right there, with that satellite.'

It all clicked for Eve. She had long pondered how the Rocket would have been capable of reaching a faraway planet like Earth. But if it was only going to orbit, then it was a much more reasonable and achievable goal. *If the Rocket even worked,* Eve reminded herself, remembering the poor diagnostics returned by the cores.

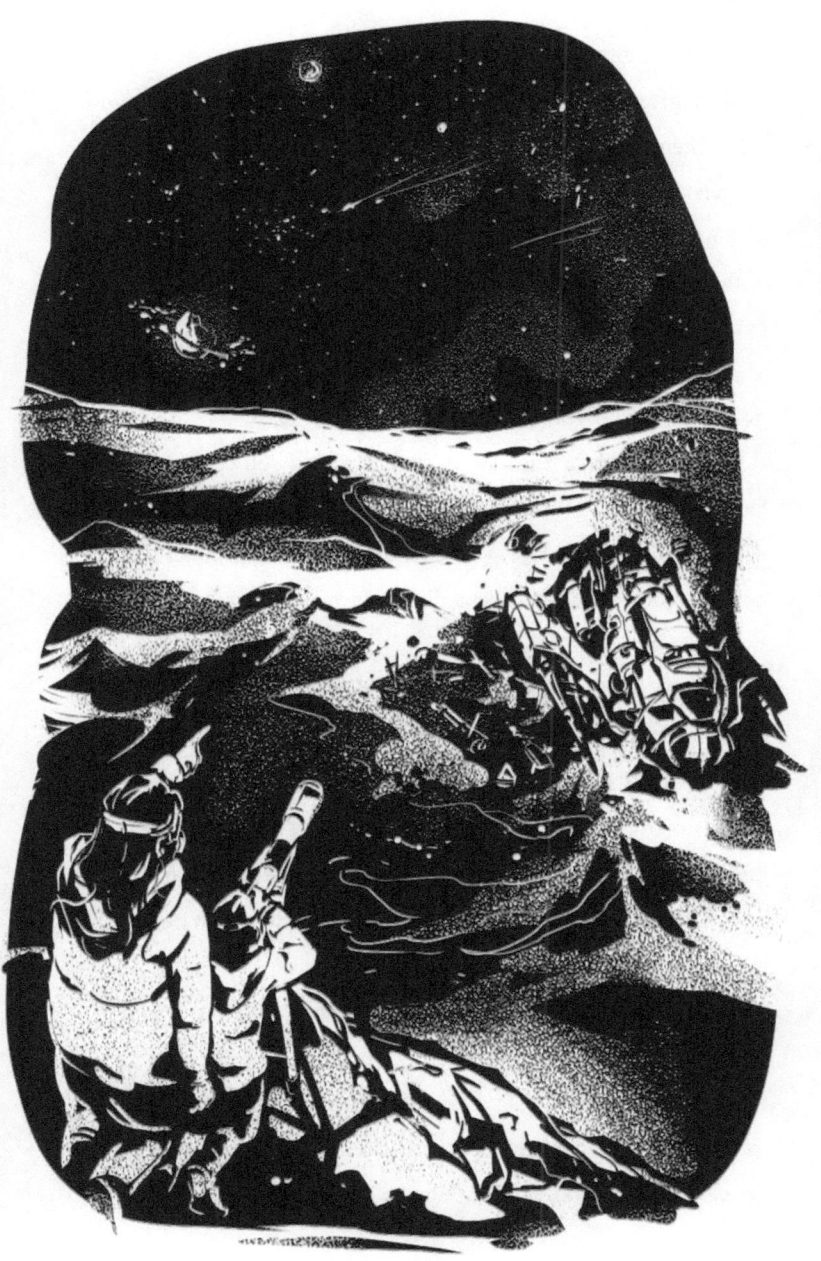

Nisma sighed. 'Eve,' she said with a wary tone.

Eve grunted, looking up at her mother. She knew what *that* voice meant.

Nisma averted her gaze, looking off somewhere in the distance. 'Now. I *know* you enjoyed exploring the *Eternity* with your father yesterday, but you *need* to know that was an exception.'

Eve raised an eyebrow. She did not like where this was going. 'What do you mean?'

Nisma shook her head a little. 'I'm afraid you can't go back.'

Her words filled Eve with disappointment. She could not believe what she was hearing. *So, this was why you wanted to come out here with me?*

A deep fire burned up inside her. 'Why not?' Eve demanded. 'I've never been allowed to scavenge before. You've always kept me *inside* while Dad went on his own!'

Nisma took a knee, meeting her daughter eye to eye. 'I know, but I was *truly* scared that I would lose you, and if that were to happen, I don't think I would be able to live with myself.'

Eve pushed away, furious. 'But I *really* enjoyed it. Dad did *too!*'

'I'm sorry, Eve,' Nisma said, shaking her head and rising to her feet. 'You can't go back.' She turned and made off for the cave. 'Don't stay out too long.'

Eve stood still, dumbfounded. She could not believe the double whammy she had just been dealt. She looked back at the *Eternity* and then up at the sky where the satellite was hidden amongst the stars. She wanted to say something back, but found only hate-filled words. She held her tongue.

If there was one thing that was easy to find on Concord Prime, it was water. Innumerable pools of it, formerly Rain that had been neutralised and cursed to stagnation, dotted the low points between the melted hills of the planet. Though no longer as dangerous as its recently precipitated form, these pools still held acidity levels far above what could be considered suitable for consumption by any living creature. However, with careful monitoring and application of further neutralising compounds, this water could become drinkable.

Eve had found herself at one of these pools along with Eli and a small ATV attached to a trailer housing a water tank. She waltzed around the edge of the moonlit water, kicking the occasional pebble into it and watching the small waves from its submersion emanate out across the calm surface. A niggling sense of overexposure nipped at Eve's subconscious, constantly keeping her alert of the dangers of wandering outside the safety of the Rover. She glanced over to Eli a short distance away, who was on a knee holding a strip of paper in the water. A little pH testing kit lay beside him, folded out to show a collection of hundreds more strips of paper.

The pool was modest, only twenty metres across and probably no deeper than a metre or two, but a combination of ground composition and location further downhill had allowed it to hold water of much lower acidity than all other pools in the area. Because of this, it was gifted the name the Spring.

Eve rubbed her gloved hands together and shivered a little. The temperatures around the pools were often considerably colder than the surrounding areas, and she had donned extra layers as per her father's suggestion, but the cold still managed to seep its way in to molest her skin. She kicked another pebble into the pool and watched it sink and vanish from her torchlight.

'Tell you what, Eve,' Eli said, keeping his eye on the strip of paper in his hand, 'all that Rain yesterday has left plenty of water lying around. We're gonna have enough for both the electrolyser and aquaponics for *months*.' He rose to his feet and shook a few rogue droplets from the strip of paper, its original yellow tinge having turned green. 'pH five. That's good enough for the filters. Bring the hose over, please.'

Eve nodded. 'Okay.' She jogged over to the trailer, pulled a length of hose from it and ran it over to Eli who took it and dipped it into the water.

'Thank you,' he said, flipping a switch on the hose nozzle.

A small pump on the trailer activated and water began to rise up out of the pool and flow along the hose into the tank. Content that the tank was filling, Eli left the hose to its work and arched his back with a grunt, cracking several vertebrae.

He sighed and took a seat on a nearby mound of rock, balling up the strip of paper and tossing it aside. 'So, Eve. How'd you enjoy exploring the *Eternity* the other day?'

The question perplexed Eve, and she recalled the conversation she'd had with Nisma the day before. Was he probing her for something? Was he working for Nisma? Eve could not say for certain. Though she did thoroughly enjoy wandering around its endless tunnels, Central Park and the bridge, despite the abrupt ending due to the Rain. She figured it could not have been of any harm if she said what she *really* thought about it. *It might even help them change their mind if I tell them I enjoyed it,* she thought.

'It was awesome,' Eve said, hoping she sounded convincing enough.

Eli chuckled. 'Thought you'd like it. Next time I'll show you the stadium where we used to play sports. I was a *mad* tight end on the gridiron back in the day.'

His choice of words made Eve raise an eyebrow. *Wait, so Mom* did *change her mind?*

'Next time?'

Eli tilted his head, confused. 'Yeah. Next time. Why? What's wrong? You didn't like it?'

Eve shook her head and held up her hands. 'Oh, no. It's just...' She trailed off, not wanting to say anything further.

He doesn't know? she thought. *I thought he knew. Shouldn't he know?* She was just as confused as Eli was.

'Just what?' Eli urged sternly, hoping to get Eve to spit out the last few words.

Eve's heart skipped a beat. *Did I say something wrong?*

She swallowed, but found her mouth parched. 'It's just… Mom said I wasn't allowed to go anymore because it was dangerous.'

Eli shook his head in disbelief. He scratched his head. 'This is the first *I've* heard of this.'

His tone broiled with a restrained anger that made Eve anxious. She never liked it when her father got angry. Eli shot to his feet, making her jump.

'I go in there all the time while *she* stays in the Rover,' he said, anger rising. 'Too dangerous? *Too dangerous*?!'

'I-I'm sorry,' Eve apologised, hoping to defuse the situation. 'I thought she told you.'

Eli pointed at Eve. 'You're telling me *she* thinks it's too dangerous?' He motioned around at the landscape, the endless rise and falls of melted mountains caught under a perpetual blackness dotted with white stars and a fractured moon. 'Look at where we *fucking* live!' he roared. 'This whole planet is the definition of hell, and *she* thinks the *Eternity* is too dangerous?!' He sent the pH kit flying with a strong kick, scattering the hundreds of strips of paper into the wind. 'What the *fuck* does she know?!'

A few moments of silence followed. Eve was frozen in terror, too afraid to even breathe. She could feel her heart thump furiously in her chest, a hair away from bursting free.

She kept her eyes locked on her father in a petrified stare. He had barely moved since his outburst. She watched him peel his goggles off and rub at his brow before placing them back over his eyes. She wished with all her soul that she had never even opened her mouth.

Eli eventually shook his head and shot a glance at Eve. She kept still, her motionless form almost blending in with the rocks around her. He coughed and Eve swore she heard a muffled snort through her father's mask. His aggressive stance slowly melted away and he looked to the ground, at the dozens of paper strips that littered the rocks, not wanting to meet his daughter in the eyes.

'I-I'm really sorry, Eevee. I—' he started before cutting himself off. He knelt down and started to pick up the strips one at a time, not looking even remotely in Eve's direction.

Eve watched for a while before finding herself also on the ground picking up pieces of the testing kit. Not a single word was spoken between them until their return to the Rover.

CHAPTER FOUR

To describe Spud as a robot or automaton of some kind would
have been an overstatement. The mountain of wires, cables
and components that comprised his physical form resembled a
haphazard pile of scrap more than anything else. The only
discernible feature was his head—a crude, metallic skull
stripped of all aesthetic plating. It certainly was not much to
look at, but it *was* merely a prototype body—a temporary
housing for Spud's critical hardware to allow him to operate at
the simplest level until Eve could manufacture something
more permanent.

Like the organs in a person, Eve had originally concluded
upon finishing his initial schematic, noting the similarities
between the alloys of Spud and her own flesh. The idea
proved to be more accurate than she'd thought, having given
some time to ponder it further; the wires were his blood
vessels, the electricity running through them was his blood, his
optics were his eyes, the microphones were his ears, chemical

receptors were his nose, a speaker was his mouth, the processor was his brain and his programming his DNA. He would have every sense a human would have, barring taste, and function very much like a human would.

At least that was Eve's plan, should he actually work. She had big plans for Spud, but so far, she could not even get his most basic form to function. Following a fault-finding, Eve had discovered that his processor and programming were utterly incompatible with each other, resulting in the former's short circuiting. It was the latest in a long string of failures that Eve had fought through, but she was not ready to give up. Since then, she had made some adjustments, lowering the power intake for the time being. It meant Spud would be slow, dumb for lack of a better word, but at least he would be alive.

Eve was at her workbench, fiddling with a set of tweezers she hoped Spud could use for manipulators once he finally activated. Her computer blinked beside her, depicting a progression bar that trickled ever closer to full. She had remained in her room for the most part since her return from the Spring, making the final tunings to both Spud's body and his programming. She had tried to keep the thoughts of the last few cycles from distracting her, but had quickly found it to be futile, her mind constantly casting itself back to her conversation with Nisma then to what occurred with Eli while they were collecting water. She did this over and over again, pausing, rewinding and fast forwarding her memories in hopes of finding something that she could have done better. There were plenty, of course, but she knew she could do nothing to alter what had already been set in the stone of time no matter how much she wanted.

A beep from her computer pulled Eve from her thoughts. She placed the tweezers down and spun round to face the monitor, which informed her of the successful upload of the Spud OS. She smiled, running a hand through her straight black hair with relief. 'All right, took long enough.'

Her hands dug through the Spud Mountain, searching for the motherboard. After a short excavation, her hand came up with what she desired. Eve felt her pulse skyrocket as she laid a finger against the power switch. She paused, running the path and order of component start-up through her head to ensure everything was ready. She did not want to blow another processor, or worse. *Won't know unless I turn it on,* she told herself.

'Here goes,' she swallowed, flipping the switch.

The motherboard hummed into life, and lights illuminated all across Spud's form. Components fired up and instantly began self-diagnostics, returning positive response after positive response. Eve's spirits rose with every successful bleep and click. Before long all auxiliary components had fired up, leaving only the processor. Eve prayed with all her will, not daring to break eye contact with the electronics. *Come on, Spud. You can do it.*

A light illuminated beside the processor, indicating a successful diagnostic.

Eve nearly leapt out of her seat. 'Oh my god.' She scrambled for Spud's head, scooping it up into her hands with his optics staring into her eyes. 'I'll be the first thing you see, buddy,' Eve said, giddily. 'Welcome to Concord, your home.'

Spud's optics glowed a deep red, self-diagnostics activating and returning optimistic readings. He instantly took in the first details of the world around him and stored the first droplets of information as it flowed in.

Sparks burst out from the processor in a miniaturised fireworks display.

Eve watched in dismay as Spud's optics dulled and returned to black before her. 'Shit!' she cursed, dropping Spud's head into his pile and slumping back into her chair. 'Come on, Spud. Work with me.'

Eve rubbed her brow, wincing a bit when she crossed over her Mark. *So close. We were so close. All this time and effort and we are this close.* She had long since lost track of the amount of time she had invested in Spud; split between coding the baseline framework on which his self-learning program would sprout from and manufacturing his physical chassis itself. She had looted countless components from disused Rover parts, Nisma's Rocket refuse and the occasional scraps Eli would bring back from the *Eternity* for her. These all had quickly overran her workbench and spilled over onto the floor of her room, something that both her parents had urged her to clean up, but Eve had dutifully neglected to do so, not willing to part with a single bolt or wire until she was finished. And, oh, she was *so* close to finishing. She straightened back up and picked up Spud's head, looking him directly in his dead optics. *I'm not giving up on you, Spud,* she swore. *I'll find a way to make you work.*

An object drew her attention from Spud's optics, and she glanced over at something beside the family photograph on the workbench. It was the odd processor she had picked up from the *Eternity.* Eve had completely forgotten about it. She laid Spud down and took up the processor, instantly noting its similarities with the other processor that just got fried. *It certainly* looks *like a processor,* she thought, spinning the component in her hand. *What's it supposed to be?* Her eyes casted back to the photograph with her mother and father looking up at her. *Would Mom or Dad know?*

Eve did not like talking to her parents about Spud. When she initially proposed her idea to her parents, they were sceptical and assumed it to be either some form of childlike text-to-speech talking program at best or a waste of valuable resources at worst. Nisma had immediately taken up banners with the latter, believing the time and effort Eve was investing in Spud could be put to better use, such as assisting her with the Rocket.

Eli was slightly better, having initially sided with Nisma, but slowly transitioning to the former through amiable encouragement and invested interest. Eve liked that he showed attention to her work, even if it was just a painfully obvious humouring to not dissuade his daughter from her hobby.

Despite their lack of support, Eve knew her parents were both very knowledgeable with the systems of the *Eternity* and might be able to shed some light on the purpose of the queer component she held in her hand.

Eve sighed and rose to her feet, keeping the piece on her as she opened the door into the common room. She called out to both Nisma and Eli several times, tracking a path from the common room, to their bedroom, to the medbay and downstairs into the cargo bay and aquaponics chamber. There was no one. Eve ascended the ladder back into the common room and pondered, *Where are they?* They could have been outside, though Eve could not remember hearing the airlock activate, so they were definitely *inside* the Rover somewhere.

A muffled murmur drifted down from the cockpit, an intense conversation smothered by steel walls and an attempt at restraint. It piqued Eve's interest. She carefully placed the processor down onto the dining table and drew near to the stairs, keeping her steps quiet to hide her approach. She knew it was no good when her parents spoke behind locked doors; it meant they were discussing things that were not supposed to be destined for her ears. But their attempts at obscuring their words proved only to captivate Eve further.

She climbed the stairs in quick succession, keeping her feet light and silent, coming up to the closed door that would open up into the cockpit. *Locked,* Eve thought, noting the padlock symbol displayed on the screen beside it. She leaned in close, pressing her ear against the cold steel and cupping her hands around it, but found the conversation on the other side of the door to still be too difficult to discern.

Eve wrinkled her nose and pulled away from the door, sliding quietly over to the padlocked screen beside it. *I'll use the cameras then,* she told herself. She had long since mastered the ability to patch into the Rover's internal camera network though she never actively used it out of fear of getting in trouble. But the events of the last few cycles and the evident slow-boiling tension between her parents had pushed Eve's anxiety and curiosity to critical levels and she desired closure.

A few taps on the screen and a quick navigation through several submenus later and a small grainy video feed of the cockpit popped up. The video's lighting was subpar at best, the power into the cockpit having been turned off and the only source of light being a lonesome illumination dome built into the roof. The bitrate was horrible and the volume was almost non-existent, but it was good enough for Eve to tell what was being said.

Eve watched the video feed in silent anticipation. She could make out two figures in the cockpit. One of them, obviously Eli by his gait, paced up and down the cockpit in an impatient prowl. His eyes were locked onto Nisma who was seated on the pilot's control console with her arms viced beside her.

'She's a smart girl, Nis. You can't keep her caged up inside the Rover her entire life,' Eli said in a stern pixelated tone. 'She *needs* to learn how to scavenge the *Eternity* on her own, because one day, I won't be able to.'

'I'm *not* trying to,' Nisma retorted with a slightly aggressive rise in her demeanour. 'But, the ship has been eaten away by the Rain for years now. It's only a matter of time before it falls apart. I'm just trying to keep her safe.'

Eli shook his head, visibly dismissive of Nisma's words. 'Safe from what? You *do* realise we're living on a death planet?'

His words echoed the thoughts in Eve's head. *Exactly, what are you keeping me safe from?* she inquired silently, thankful that Eli shared her sentiments on the matter.

Nisma rubbed her brow, a common tick when she grew frustrated, but she strived to maintain the emotional high ground against her husband. 'Not for long,' she replied calmly. 'Once we find the replacement cores, we'll be long gone.'

'Gone *where?* That satellite?' Eli tutted. 'How do you even know it *is* a satellite? Whenever I've looked at it, it was just a blurry smudge of grey stuff. It could be a chunk of the fucking moon for all we know.'

His tone was unstable and Eve could tell he was on the brink of an emotional outburst.

Nisma was also nearing the end of her rope. 'It's better than staying here,' she grumbled.

Eli stopped his pacing and let out a mocking chuckle, thrusting a finger out towards the darkened cave where the

Rocket would be standing. 'Staying *here* is better than dying in orbit! That's if we're not killed on the way by that pile of rubbish you call a rocket!'

Eve's eyes widened. *Dying?*

Nisma leapt to her feet and defiantly stared Eli down. 'It's better than a lifetime scrounging for scraps in this shithole!'

Eli marched up to her and met her glare, planting a firm finger on her chest. '*You're* not even the one doing the fucking scrounging! *I am!*'

Nisma did not back down and spat venom through gritted teeth. '*We* don't belong here. *Eve* doesn't belong here. And, one way or another, with or *without* your help, *I'll* be getting her *off* this godforsaken rock.'

Her words rattled Eve. She knew that the two of them never particularly agreed on the Rocket project, but they always managed to bring it together in the end to work towards a common goal. *It's what families do, right?*

Eli held her gaze for a few moments before tutting, his suspicions confirmed. 'So, that's how it is? You have *no* objections to me risking *my* life every time I enter that ship to find parts for you. Yet you don't trust me, for *one second*, to be a father to my daughter?'

He paused and Eve thought she could see the grimace on his face.

'I'm just a disposable asset to you.'

His words tore through both Nisma and Eve like rusted blades. Eve was bewildered. He was Nisma's husband, her other half, her soulmate. How could she ever think of him in such a demeaning and materialistic way. *Was that what she really thought of him? Just another piece of machinery? Something to be used up and thrown away?* Eve watched Nisma shake her head and avert her gaze away from her husband in a manner that Eve struggled to place between disgust or guilt.

Eli huffed, his wife's reaction proving to be all the confirmation he needed. 'I knew it.'

He turned and marched towards the door. The moment his back was turned Nisma glared daggers into him, but said nothing more. Eve could barely muster a thought, an overwhelming feeling of dread having washed over her. The scene that had unfurled before her almost overwhelmed her brain's bandwidth.

Her heart lurched at the sound of the door's locking mechanisms grinding free. *Oh, no.* In a panic, she closed the video feed and scurried down the stairs to her bedroom, grabbing the unusual processor on the way. She closed the door behind her as quickly as its hydraulics would allow and, as her door finally slid shut, she caught a glimpse of the entrance into the cockpit opening and the figure of her father appearing from behind it.

Eve bounced around her room and dug around for something to put in her hands, hoping to give the illusion that she had been working on Spud the entire time. She scooped up the tweezers she held before and probed it for loose screws.

Her mind ran through the entire conversation over and over again, and she felt herself grow more and more depressed with each playthrough. *How could you say things like that?* she thought, tears welling in her eyes. *You're family.* A knock on her door made her jump with a suppressed yelp.

'Eevee, you in there?' Eli's voice asked from the other side in a cautious manner, a complete backflip from how he was only a few seconds prior.

He saw me... Eve grimaced. The door opened before she could give a response, revealing Eli standing on the other side.

'Hey,' he started, looking around awkwardly, 'it all right for me to come in?'

Eve did not answer, pretending she was preoccupied with her work. She glanced at him from the corner of her eye, silently wishing her father would leave her alone.

Eli sighed and entered, closing the door behind him. He shot a glance up at the cockpit as the door was closing. The cockpit was sealed, Nisma not having made any attempt to follow him.

'I know you were listening, Eve,' he said, not keen on beating around the bush. 'It's okay. You're not in trouble.'

'You were fighting,' Eve uttered, hating every word she spoke.

Eli tried to deflect her claim. 'Fighting? No. Your mother and I were just having a talk, that's all.'

His poor excuse did not trick Eve. She knew what she saw. 'It *sounded* like a fight. You and Mom were angry.'

Eli languished. 'Well. Sometimes your mother and I get a bit annoyed with each other. But it's okay. We've sorted everything out now.'

'Really?'

'Yep.'

His answer did not entirely convince Eve. *It didn't sound 'sorted' out.* She halted her feigned work on the tweezers and placed them on the workbench.

She turned her head and glanced at Eli with a questioning, raised eyebrow. 'Is it true what you said?' she asked, locking stern brown eyes with her father's clear blue. 'That the Rocket won't work?'

Her question took her father aback and he worded his response slowly and carefully. 'Um. Well... I wouldn't *say* that it was true, Eevee. You know your mother is the one in charge of the Rocket, not me.' He gave a sincere smile. 'She's a *lot* smarter than I am with those things, so if she says it'll work, then it'll work.'

He casted a quick glance across his daughter's room, no doubt judging its messy state and Eve awaited the inevitable berating of its sorry condition. His eyes traced onto her workbench where a mountain of electronics morphed over half the workspace and crept up the side of the built-in monitor. It took him a second to spot the small-framed family photograph beside the monitor, half buried in the scrap. His eyes held the photo in view for a moment before drifting on to Spud's head at the foot of the mountain. Spud stared back at him with blank optics.

Eli nodded at the head. 'Say, is this the project you've been working on?'

Eve followed his motion and landed on Spud's head. She did not expect him to inquire about Spud. 'Oh, yeah,' she said, rising out of her chair to scoop Spud's head up into her hands. 'This is Spud.'

The name made Eli chuckle a little. 'Spud, huh? Why'd you call it that?'

'Because *he* kinda looks like mashed potatoes,' Eve explained, straining the emphasis on the 'he.'

Eli chuckled again. 'I see. Does *he* work?'

Eve shook her head, lowering Spud's head. 'He did for a bit earlier, but he keeps burning out the processors I find for him.' She took out the destroyed processor and handed it to Eli.

He glazed it over, running a finger over several burn marks. 'Hm. So what's the problem?' he asked.

Eve tapped her chin, not surprised that he missed the obvious. 'I think he's drawing too much power for the processors to handle.'

Eli nodded. 'So, you need stronger processors?'

Eve shrugged at his indisputable answer. 'I guess so.'

A rumble from deep within the Rover made the both of them freeze. Although she had never operated the Rover herself, a lifetime living within its walls had given Eve an innate knowledge of the Rover's inner workings; it was starting up. She glanced to Eli, who was already out the door and marching across the common room, having also come to the same conclusion.

'Nis?!' he shouted, bounding up the stairs to the cockpit. 'What are you doing?!'

Eve leapt up and scurried after him, stopping at the bottom of the stairs and peering up its length. Eli had halted at the door and entered a code into the console, yielding a negative response. The Rover lurched, making both Eve and Eli stumble. The tell-tale sounds of wheels grinding rock to dust informed Eve that they were now in motion.

Eli slammed a fist against the cockpit door. 'Nis, open the door!'

A piercing crackling radiated throughout the Rover. It took Eve a moment to realise that it was the Rover's seldomly used speaker system activating.

'We are *this* close to freedom, Eli,' Nisma's voice boomed through the speaker system, 'and I will *not* let our best chance of survival rot away like everything else on this damned planet.'

'You got some nerve,' Eli growled.

'You're normally pretty keen when it comes to digging around in the filth of our dead past, Eli. What's wrong with me wanting to take a dip for once?'

It was a long, tense journey to the *Eternity*. One that Eve rode out in the privacy of her room. Outside, Eli argued ferociously with Nisma, who responded with just as much cruelty. Eve was quick to disconnect the speaker that was installed in her room in the hope of sound proofing herself from the rest of the Rover, but to no avail. She tried to distract herself by working on Spud, but it proved to be fruitless. She concluded that these walls, no matter how thick they were, what they were made of, or how much sound they kept out, there was always a little bit that always snuck through.

Her parents fighting was not a new concept to Eve. She had heard dozens of them echo throughout the walls of the Rover, but this one was different. It seeped in through every crack and crevice into her room. The words. The names. The accusations. They all stung Eve as much as they did their intended targets. She wished it would stop with all her heart, her eyes never straying far from the photograph beside her monitor, but she knew it would not.

After what felt like an eternity, the Rover grinded to a halt and shook Eve from the daydream she was in. She glanced out the porthole to see the towering form of the *Eternity* before her. She swallowed, already anticipating the conflict that was surely to erupt once her mother emerged from the Rover's cockpit.

Eve sat at her desk, ears pricked, dreading the inevitable onslaught that would erupt once her mother opened up the cockpit door. She held her breath when she heard the door's hydraulics activate followed by steps down the steel staircase into the common room. They were slower than normal and placed with more caution and forethought. Something shifted in the common room, which Eve presumed to be her father. He did nothing else, at least nothing audible.

'I'm going,' Nisma growled from the other side of Eve's door, a slight waver in her voice, 'and there's nothing you can do to stop me.'

Eve waited for a response from Eli. For a moment there was nothing, then there were footsteps that travelled over to the ladder and down into the cargo bay. Then nothing again. Eve did not know what to think of the situation. The silence was uncanny, yet she also welcomed it in a way. There was no yelling. Perhaps a silent agreement between them had been reached? At least that was what she hoped for.

A resonating hiss sounded from below which Eve instantly identified as the airlock. She slid to her feet, keeping her steps as quiet as possible, and peered out the porthole. The *Eternity* laid before her, its imposing form blocking out all but the highest of stars, and its shadow blanketing the Rover in its entirety.

A lonely flashlight originating below Eve surveyed the terrain, its beam quickly being swallowed up by the dark. It started to move, floating ominously away from the Rover and towards the *Eternity*. Eve could not see the body that carried it, but assumed it to be Nisma. She watched it in silence as it entered the maw of the great decaying vessel. It froze and casted its beam back towards the Rover, making Eve instinctively drop below the porthole. She raised her head back up when the light rotated back around and went on its merry way before disappearing entirely behind the great steel walls.

Eve pulled herself away from the porthole and made for the door. It slid open to show an empty room. At least Eve initially thought it was empty until she noticed the still form of Eli sitting at the dining table with his head lying on its surface.

'Dad?' she asked, hoping not to trigger a violent response.

Eli sighed and kept his head on the table; she knew he hated it when she saw him like this.

'It's all right, Eevee,' he grumbled. 'Your mother's just gone to get parts for the Rocket. She'll be back soon.'

Eve was about to say something, but stopped when her father rose to his feet. He scratched at his face, a muzzle already taking shape, and made for the door into his and Nisma's bedroom. He tried to avert his face from Eve, but she was still able to catch a glimpse. He looked tired, worn through, beaten down, yet he had not done any physical work to Eve's knowledge. It concerned her, but before she could think of anything to say, Eli disappeared into his room and locked the door behind him.

Returning to her own room, Eve sat back down at her workbench. She leaned back and tried to process all that had transpired. It was an impossible task, and one that she quickly gave up. A depressing feeling dropped on her, a sense of loneliness and worthlessness that she wished she could talk to someone about. She raised her head, and her eyes met the lifeless optics of Spud. Eve swallowed and took up his head.

'You're a real pain, Spud,' she tutted, beholding Spud with weary eyes. 'You know that, right?'

She waited for an answer, and of course, none came. She shook her head and glanced at the motherboard, focussing on the empty processor mount. It aggravated her. *I'm so close. I just need one more processor.* She looked out the porthole, at the dark form of the *Eternity,* then back to Spud. It gave her an idea.

The door slid open, and Eve peered out, confirming that there were no signs of life. Taking careful steps, she made her way to the ladder and descended down into the cargo bay, making sure to land quietly at the bottom. After another scan of the area, Eve moved for the airlock and closed herself in. She engaged the door lock and began to suit up. *If* she's *going in, then I can too.*

It sensed her presence the moment she entered its domain. Through microscopic lenses it watched the small human trace a haphazard trail through the peripheral corridors of sector 7-G. Anxiety was plastered across her face, something plainly visible even with the mask and goggles fastened across it and it mirrored the larger human who passed through a while before. It was strange to see more than one human exploring the *Eternity*.

Normally, they only send the largest one, known as 'Eli,' but it had failed to find his location, meaning Eli was, most likely, still aboard their vehicle. Definitely an unusual occurrence, something that culminated with a surprising lack of radio activity.

It grumbled to itself, not liking the rogue factors one bit. *+Is there something wrong with their radios? Interference maybe? Or did they forget to turn their radios back on like last time.+*

It scoured the network of cameras, lights, consoles, doors and anything else connected to the *Eternity's* mainframe that could provide useful information, eventually locating the other large human inside one of the dozens of escape pod hangars. That human, which it had learned was called 'Nisma,' had managed to cut open one of the dormant escape pods and disappeared inside. It doubted the human was trying to use the escape pods, their activation requiring an administrator approval that would never come. That is, save for one instance, where it permitted an activation just for them to drag away the extracted escape pod like a predatory animal with its prey. It knew what the escape pod was intended for, and it knew that it was also the best chance for it to escape off-world.

Having quickly grown bored of watching Nisma cut the escape pod apart, it turned its attention back to the smaller human; the one that it was *really* interested in. It could not pinpoint a title for the little creature, and she was not present on any demographic databases or census reports that it could locate. It then concluded that the little human must have been born *after* the crash, most likely as the child of Eli and Nisma. This was cross-referenced with Nisma's medical reports which stated her pregnancy being four months into fruition at the time of the crash.

That proved to be an irritation. For all intents and purposes, the child was off-the-record; something that was a source of concern, initially, as it was unable to source any meaningful pieces of information on the creature. But it all proved to be misplaced after the discovery of her youthful naivety, something that could be manipulated, and its technological aptitude—a valued skill if one sought to flee off-world.

Though, the same could not be said about the child's navigational skills, and since entering the walls of the *Eternity* she had done little more than approach then confound herself with a four-way intersection. It watched closely, silently urging the child to take the rightmost passage towards Central Park and their eventual unification. It quickly became apparent that the little human had no idea where she was going, but with a helpful flicker of a light here and a subtle opening and closing of a doorway there, she was slowly guided on to the right path.

Eve felt she was making progress now. Having initially struggled with recognising the correct path to take, she was confident she was on approach to Central Park. Since she possessed very little knowledge of the layout of the *Eternity*, Eve had concluded that the bridge would have been the best place to search first with potentially other places if she acquired a map or schematic.

She had almost forgotten how dark the tunnels of the *Eternity* were—an inescapable, suffocating darkness that swallowed up the light from her flashlight as quickly as it came out. She kept a hand near the wall, letting her gloved fingers run across its cold metallic surface to give her the slightest sense of spatial awareness and direction. She had been walking blindly for the most part, following the occasional blip of light that may come up in her travels. It was not the best solution, but it was the only means she could work with. Eve tutted, remembering Eli's words regarding how his paths through the *Eternity* always seemed to manifest before him like they were to her. *Odd.*

Despite this, Eve swallowed a mouthful of anxiety. The initial rebellious surge in her chest had long since been worn away by the claustrophobic black. Second thoughts began to float into her mind: *What if I get lost? What if I can't find anything? What if I get hurt?* She pushed the thought out of her head and focussed on moving forwards. *I'm this close, Spud. I'm this close.*

The concerns stuck to her like a stubborn stain. Her heart thumped in her ears, almost draining out the ominous whirring of the distant machines that still laboured to keep the *Eternity* alive and functioning to some degree. Her mask clung to her face, stretching and relaxing with her breaths. Eve could tell she was taking in as much air as the filters could physically allow. It troubled her, and she prayed that she would not need to exhort herself any more than she had to.

CHAPTER FIVE

Eve tried to mask her steps as best as possible, her hard-soled boots proving quite difficult to disguise with the dull droning ambience of the *Eternity* and the acoustic nature of its tunnels. She also paid close attention to the radio in her ear, listening for any activity or even a stray splash of static that may hint at her discovery. So far there had been nothing from either the Rover or Nisma, which served to further encourage Eve's belief that her absence had not been detected. *With any luck, I'll be back before anyone notices.*

After what felt like an eternity, walking blindly in the dark, Eve's eyes caught a hint of ambient light from the corridor ahead. Her pace quickened, picking up into a light jog. The light drew closer, illuminating more and more of the tight corridor with every step. Eve could feel her claustrophobia fade away as the light revealed more of the space around her. First were vague outlines, then basic shapes, then depth, then colour. The light was strange, definitely not that of a computer monitor or console display, yet it was familiar at the same time.

A bend materialised in the corridor ahead, the source of the light coming from beyond it. When Eve rounded the corner, she stopped in her tracks and covered her eyes. A beam of light seared into her flesh, illuminating her olive skin to a radiance and casting a hard shadow behind her. It took a while for her eyes to adjust, having been so adept at operating in the dark, and for a moment Eve feared she had gone blind.

Before her stood the imposing figure of a tree, its body reaching out of the ground like a brown pillar. It creaked and groaned like an overstressed rebar as it flexed in the breeze. A miniature sun suspended above it drenched the immobile being in the warm, blinding light. Eve had never seen anything so bright, so intense. It was an exposure so powerful that, compounded with her close proximity, rendered the floodlights that illuminated the Rocket to little more than weak diodes in comparison.

Despite this it held a strangely warming and soothing aura about it that resonated with Eve at both a cellular and primal level. She took in a deep breath, as deep as her mask would allow, and let the warmth sink through her clothes into her body to penetrate every layer of her being with its splendour. She fought the urge to stare directly into the source, instead settling for the green hues that glowed from the innumerable finger-length appendages that draped the tree like the hairs on her head. *They're even better up close,* she thought, pacing forwards to get a better observation.

When she was near enough, she reached her hand out and planted it against the tree's sturdy trunk. The lack of texture was a disappointment to Eve until she realised her glove was still on. Peeling it off, she tried again and noted an immediate improvement. The trunk was rough yet had some give if Eve applied enough pressure and was riddled with minute crevices and mounds scattered across its form. It was warm, heated by the powerful lamp above it to ward off the frigid cold. Eve noticed the lack of a heartbeat. *Do these things even have blood?* she pondered.

Her curiosity appeased for the moment, Eve moved to step back, but felt something rustle against her boots. She looked down and found herself standing amongst a sea of green blades interwoven with each other. She dropped to a knee and cast a hand over the khaki blades, feeling their edges graze against her skin. They were sharp, yet they yielded to her hand as she passed over them and never once cut her skin. She stopped her pass and pinched one of the blades between her finger and thumb. A waxy substance scrubbed off onto her. It perplexed Eve, and she rubbed it between her fingers. She considered squeezing one of the green blades and picking it out from its roots, but stopped herself. *If these things are alive, wouldn't they feel pain, too?* she asked herself, straightening up. She lifted one of her boots up to see the crushed remnants of dozens of the blades beneath it. A pang of empathy washed over her, and Eve retreated back to where the soil transformed into metal. She watched the tree for a few moments longer as she pulled her glove back over her hand. *He talked a lot about how much better things were before the crash,* she thought, her mind cast back to her first trip into the *Eternity* with Eli.

A strange hollow feeling welled up inside her, and she screwed up her face in frustration. 'If only I was there to see it,' she grumbled, pacing around to take in her surroundings.

She deduced that she had found her way to the bottom level of Central Park, which proved to be a problem since she was intending to find the bridge. Her eyes scanned the horizon, hoping to spot the walkway that Eli and herself had taken to reach her envisioned destination, but found it to be a fruitless endeavour.

She made out dozens of walkways and staircases that lined the perimeter walls of the park, and those were just the ones she could see before they were drowned out by distance and darkness. Most appeared to be in good condition, but some had already met their fate as twisted piles of metal rubble several storeys beneath their intended mountings—no doubt the result of Rain exposure. They were joined by large segments of the roof along with the great pillars that supported them, all having been eaten away by Concord's volatile weather, leaving great holes that permitted the starry sky to peer inside the *Eternity's* entrails. It was a sight that Eve had only managed a vague glimpse of from her original viewpoint several storeys up. *It's so much worse down here,* she noted, giving the ruined pillars and roofing a more prudent second passing.

All around the wreckage were great mounds of silver which Eve believed to be the remnants of those same great pillars and walkways that took the brunt of the Rain and melted into the slag that pooled around their fallen corpses. It initially reminded Eve of poorly executed oxy-acetylene weld lines before she traced a new connection to the Mark on her head. *Metal or skin, it's all the same,* Eve concluded, picturing her flesh melting off the bone and slopping to the ground as an androgynous pile of ooze like the metallic wounds before her. *Like the nightmare...* The thought greatly disturbed Eve, and she felt sick to the stomach. She shook the pictures away, but she knew they were bound to return at an inconvenient time.

She pulled her mind back to Nisma's words regarding the state of the ship and could not help, but find herself nodding. *She was right,* she agreed. *If this is what happened after only a few years, what would be left in a decade or two?* The words made her hollowness widen, and she gritted her teeth in silent angst.

A distant whistle pulled Eve from her thoughts. Her heart skipped a beat, and she looked around, unsure if it was a person or merely a sound made by the rotting steel corpse she strode around in. About fifty metres away, a flickering green screen built into a console caught her eye. *That's odd,* Eve thought, immediately setting an intercept course for the anomaly.

She stopped beside the flickering console and wiped off years of dust with her glove. Its screen was choked with dead pixels and corrupted code as programs fought for supremacy on its finite display area. Strange and erratic sounds filtered through its ancient speaker as if the console was attempting to enlighten Eve of its agony. The spectacle piqued Eve's curiosity, and she looked around the device for a means to expose the electronics within. There was nothing, the majority of the console having been sealed into the wall itself and one of its side panels being blocked off by a chunky bulkhead beside it. Eve wrinkled her nose and gave the console a slap with her palm.

It proved to be all that the console needed, the physical jolt shaking free whatever gremlins had infested its system. A single text box popped up on the display and read, 'Greetings, Citizen,' as an apathetic female voice echoed the text from a small tortured speaker.

'Citizen?' Eve asked, not particularly expecting an answer from the malfunctioning console.

The text box changed to display: 'Clearance Level Seven. Unrestricted Access.' The speaker mimicked the words on the display.

An ear-splitting hissing erupted from the bulkhead beside the console. Locks unbuckled, and seals were broken. Tired hydraulics whined in agony as they thrust against the weight of the immense bulkhead. Eve took a step back, unsure of what was going to happen. She watched anxiously as the bulkhead slid open and grinded to a halt halfway open, the hydraulics calling it a day. Eve peered through the opening cautiously and was met with darkness. She cast her torch down, but found little more than a few metres of tunnel before the dark took over. Even the ambient light from the tree lamps was swallowed as quickly as her torch light.

'Hello?' she called out, her voice echoing down into the black.

The console whistled again. 'Please proceed.'

Eve squinted at the console, suspicious of a malignant purpose hidden behind the monotonous console's utterances, before returning her gaze back to the dark tunnel beyond the half-opened bulkhead. On the one hand, she had no idea where the tunnel led and, in all likelihood, could be nowhere Nisma or even Eli had ever set foot before. On the other she had already come this far for Spud, and the prospect of finding something beyond even the technology of the bridge, Rover or the Rocket proved to be very enticing to Eve.

'Please proceed,' the console repeated once again.

The console's words made Eve raise an eyebrow, its words almost sounding insistent. *I can always just come back the way I came,* she thought before she took her first step up to the bulkhead.

She passed through, instantly feeling a change of temperature and air quality. It was warm, dry, stale. Once inside she cast her torch out to the path ahead. It was dead straight for a few metres before breaking into a staircase that descended down into the depths. Eve approached the stairs and looked down its descent, her torch vanishing after the first ten steps. She was apprehensive, but her curiosity got the better of her, and she began her trek down the steps.

The stairs were slippery, coated in a strange grime or condensation of some kind. Eve instinctively reached for a handrailing, but found only walls laden with dust and a similar grime. She instead cast her torch downwards, carefully placing each step as she went. After a few dozen steps, a mist drifted in and made the steps difficult to make out. Eve could not help, but feel she was walking into hallowed ground as her feet disturbed the mist from its natural state.

'Have a pleasant trip,' the console called out, a slight smirk in its usually monotonous tone.

Eve whipped her head around, her instincts instantly flashing red warning signs. 'What?'

The bulkhead slammed shut and reengaged its locks and seals. Eve's heart skipped a beat, and she ran up to the bulkhead, nearly losing her footing on the slippery stairs.

'No!' she screamed, slamming her fists against the steel door. 'Let me out!'

The bulkhead did not budge, and Eve immediately began probing its perimeter for an access point into its interior electronics.

A distant whistle made her freeze.

'Who's there?' she called out, spinning around and pressing her back against the bulkhead.

A green light flickered far beneath her at the bottom of the stairs, submerged deep below the mist's waterline. It was another console. A distant hissing followed, trailed by the sound of metal grinding against metal. The mist wafted in response to the movement.

'Please step forward,' the far-flung console beckoned. 'Please proceed.'

Eve was unsure and casted a fleeting look at the bulkhead behind her.

'Please proceed,' the console insisted.

Eve shook her head and swallowed. *So much for going back out the way I came.*

Eli sprawled out on his bed in the top bunk and stared blankly up at the ceiling, tracing the intricate pattern of pipes, tubes and cables that raced across its matte metal surface with a finger. He had long since given up trying to get some sleep, his mind too laden with thoughts to allow rest. He pondered many things, most of which were too painful to linger on for long so he sought out the few bright spots amongst the pile.

He particularly liked the scavenging trip with Eve and he recalled her inquiry on how many people had lived in that great ship. He gave the answer of course, five hundred thousand, but he also left out plenty of information that should not be destined for his daughter's young ears.

There *were* hundreds of thousands of people on the *Eternity* when it arrived over Concord, but they were merely the latest generation to call the ship 'home.' Before them came untold epochs of people all belonging to various family lineages, cultures and heritages, most of which had sprung up during the *Eternity's* journey between the stars, but a lucky few could trace their origins back to Earth itself. In total there would have been billions of souls who wandered aboard the *Eternity* during its travels, all of them unique with their own stories to tell. But, regardless of one's individual status, they were all simply passengers blazing the way for humanity in the universe.

They were the only ones left alive to see the world that they had spent millennia crossing the stars for. They were the only ones to learn the truth of its feasibility as a place to live. They were the only ones to suffer the terrifying conclusion to their great travel. They were the epitome of ten thousand years of socio-evolution and, when it came time to finally achieve what their ancestors had set out for all those years ago, they were ready to suffer for the remainder of their lives to make the best of it. *If only they knew what awaited them,* Eli thought with a heavy heart as he pondered the innumerable people who came before him and never witnessed Concord Prime and its horrific truth. *Perhaps they might have done things differently.*

Eli's mind then trailed onto the inevitable. The initial crash most certainly killed the majority of those aboard, but there were some, like him and Nisma, who survived to make it onto the surface. Then the dangers changed from kinetic to environmental. Most that remained after the crash soon succumbed to the atmosphere; its passive acidity proved more than capable of destroying the human respiratory system atom by atom. Those that managed to survive then had to contend with the cold, meeting grim ends as frozen heaps bundled together desperately for warmth.

In all, there might have been a few dozen that made it through the gauntlet, but the final test proved to seal the fates of all but a few. The Rover, the only one in working order, was thankfully secured by Nisma's technological genius and clearance granted by her former employment as an electrical engineer officer. Accompanied by Eli and bearing their only child, they fled the wreck as soon as they could, not daring to turn back until the radiation spikes and explosions calmed down.

Eli thought of the survivors. They might have persisted for a while longer, and he often found evidence of habitation in the *Eternity* upwards of a few months after the crash. But after that, things petered out until there was nothing, but the three of them. *But for how long?* Eli grew tired of his mental gymnastics and descended to the ground.

The door into the common room opened with a whine and Eli peered out, finding no signs of activity. He glanced over to Eve's room and found it closed. A pang of guilt hit him as he recalled the events of the previous few hours. He did not know how much Eve heard of it, but with walls as thin as those in the Rover, which was built to reduce weight and not block out domestic arguments, he doubted she missed much at all.

He remembered her concerned call to him after Nisma's departure. He wanted to explain to her what happened, but could not muster the willpower to do it. So, he hid himself away, hoping to get some rest before he would tackle such a task, and of course, it failed. If anything, he was even more exhausted than before and he feared the effects that his procrastination would have in allowing the memories of the event to settle in. To become concreted in the memory of Eve that would stick with her for the rest of her life.

Eli swallowed, accepting what he had to do. *Might as well do it now.*

He closed the door behind him and strode over to Eve's bedroom, putting on a smile. 'Eve?' he said, tapping the door as firmly as a rock hitting sheet metal. 'You in there?'

There was no immediate answer. Eli waited for a moment, but nothing came. He doubted she would be asleep, at least not anymore after hearing his loud knocks. *Maybe she's ignoring me?*

'Eve, can I talk to you?' he asked, injecting as non-threatening a tone as possible.

Still no answer.

This concerned Eli. Normally Eve would have at least acknowledged his existence. Something was wrong.

'I'm coming in,' he declared, tapping on the door console to open it.

The door slid open with a hiss to reveal the infamous state of his daughter's cleanliness. Eli stepped inside and looked around, finding no signs of Eve anywhere. This perplexed him. *The cockpit?* he pondered, noting that Eve would often talk with him over the radio during previous *Eternity* expeditions and it certainly helped having someone to talk to on the longer trips. *If she wasn't working on that robot of hers that is...* he mentally added, getting a sense of pride in his daughter's handiwork. *Wish I could do something like that when I was young.*

Leaving Eve's room behind, Eli made his way to the cockpit, ascending the stairway in quick succession. He passed into the cockpit, but found it to also be devoid of life. This made Eli concerned. *If she isn't here, then where is she?* He spotted the monitor by the pilot's seat and got an idea.

He took a seat and tapped at a rudimentary keyboard built into the console. The monitor's display changed from system diagnostics to the internal camera network. Eli flicked through the cameras, passing through the common room, his and Nisma's bedroom, medbay, Eve's bedroom and more. Nothing.

Eli could feel his heart rate quicken. *Where are you, Eve?*

A horrific idea popped into his head, and he flicked through the cameras to the airlock. He struggled to see due to the grainy display, but he could just make out a single suit on the hangars. 'One suit?!' Eli exclaimed, not entirely believing what he was seeing.

He wound the recording back at eight times speed, looking for any signs of movement. After a few seconds something caught his eye. He paused, fast forwarded to the right time and watched in disbelief as Eve entered the airlock, donned her gear and departed into the black beyond.

'No,' he mumbled, pausing the replay at the moment the airlock opened and Eve was halfway out the door. 'You didn't, Eve. You didn't.' He glanced over to the radar where two blips were on display. Eli knew that one of them was Nisma, her blip located in the escape pod terminal in sector 7-G. But the other, which was tracing a path around Central Park, made his heart skip a beat. 'What are you doing?!' he roared, leaping up and dashing out of the cockpit.

Eli made it to the airlock in a flash and instantly began to don his equipment. He considered going back up to the cockpit and informing Nisma of the situation, but decided against it. *She's already dealing with enough,* he concluded, zipping up his last layer. *With any luck, she wouldn't even know we were in there.*

A few minutes later, Eli was deep within the bowels of the *Eternity.* He was taking a route that strayed a bit from the norm, several bulkheads having sealed shut for an unknown reason. *A bad time to be changing-up on me,* Eternity, he thought. He maintained his pace as best he could, his stamina being limited by his mask. After a while he started to recognise sections of the corridors. A collapsed tunnel here and a looted armoury there suggested he was on an upper echelon of the ship, something that was soon confirmed by a large archway that opened out into the old athletics arena. Running navigational information through his head, Eli determined that he would arrive at Central Park in a few minutes on one of the uppermost walkways. *That would make spotting her easier,* he thought before realising it would also run him close by where Nisma would be working in the escape pod terminal. *Hopefully she's too busy to notice.*

A good while and a lot of stairs climbing later, Eli's flashlight picked out an intersection on approach and he took the leftmost path. As he rounded the turn, a jacketed figure drifted ominously out of the dark, walking towards him.

Eli's eyes lit up. 'Eve?!'

It did not react immediately, which made Eli second-guess himself. Another moment of examining the figure as he slowed to a halt before it told him a different story. It was definitely wearing the right equipment, except it was far too big to be Eve.

'Eli?' Nisma asked quizzically, regarding Eli with her flashlight. Her arms were laden with various pieces of escape pod technology. 'What are you doing—'

'You see Eve come through here?' Eli interrupted, not overly enthusiastic about having run into Nisma.

So much for her not knowing.

Eli's words took a short while to process in Nisma's head. 'Eve? No, I…Wait, you let her go?!'

'I didn't let her go!' Eli snapped. 'She snuck out!'

'How did she manage to sneak out the airlock without *you* noticing?' Nisma remarked irritably, shuffling her armfuls of scrap around.

Eli shook his head; his patience was quickly running out. 'I don't know, but she did.'

'Dammit, Eli,' Nisma hissed. 'This is *exactly* what I was afraid of when you insisted on taking her scavenging with you. Do you know where she is, at least?'

'She was heading to Central Park when I last checked.'

Nisma sighed a breath of relief loud enough for Eli to hear. 'So, her locator is on?'

'Yes.'

'Okay,' Nisma said, no doubt thinking out the situation and the best means to solve the problem they were currently in. 'I'll go straight back to the Rover and monitor the radar. You got your radio?'

Eli nodded, tapping his ear. 'Yep.'

'Good. I'll give you updates on her location as I see them.'

'Sounds good,' Eli said, giving a thumbs up. 'Let me know when you get back.'

Without another word he slid past Nisma and continued on down the corridor in a hurry. He did not want to linger any more while Eve was still wandering the labyrinth of the *Eternity*. He also did not wish to engage in any more conversation with Nisma should she berate him further for his failure. *Yes, I made a mistake,* he said in his head, *and I'm fixing it. Like a father does.* He did not want to look back to see Nisma's judging face in his flashlight, but a single word made him freeze.

'Eli,' Nisma rumbled, her voice strong and stern.

Eli slowed up and risked a glance back, his eye catching a shred of Nisma's flashlight beam. 'Yeah?'

'Bring her back to me.' Her words were filled with barely contained rage, simmering at the brim with venom. But there was also a hint of worry in it, a tiny indicator that she did not care for what had happened, only that he would bring what she loved most in the world back to her.

Eli felt the same, but he could not think of anything worthwhile to say. He simply uttered, 'I will, Nis.'

The air was vile, almost thick enough to drink. Eve struggled to hold her breath for as long as she could before quickly exhaling and inhaling to repeat the cycle anew. She tried to avoid using her nose as much as possible, but every breath allowed a tiny sample of the smell around her to seep in and infect her nostrils. She had never smelt something so foul, a horrific scent that hung in the air in the form of the standing mist. It penetrated the filters in her mask and probed at every orifice on her face, vying for a way into her body. She had changed filters numerous times, initially believing the smell to be the result of infected filter elements, but it quickly became apparent that it was the air itself. Eve had no idea what could possibly be the source of something so repugnant. A broken septic pipe? Perhaps the air had grown so stagnant and ancient, locked away in the forgotten corridor that it developed the scent? Or, it could have been something that Eve dared not to ponder.

She glanced from side to side, seeing nothing but steel panels, piping and the gaps between them. She thought she saw something beyond the panelling between the gaps, but as soon as she could align her flashlight onto it, the mist had swallowed it whole, doomed to spend eternity in the dark. Eve shook her head and pushed on, her flashlight giving little vision beyond a few metres in the mist. Not that she needed it, the corridor was dead straight with little to no obstacles outside of the occasional protruding pipe or cable.

Every fifty metres or so, another console would stir and give Eve encouraging words to continue.

'Greetings, Citizen,' one such console bleated as she passed through the open bulkhead it was custodian over. 'Please proceed.'

Something is definitely wrong with these things, Eve thought, peering at the console from the corner of her eye as she went. She wiped at a collection of sweat droplets on her forehead and rubbed them off onto her jacket. *And why is it so hot?* The air temperature had risen gradually as she delved further into the labyrinth, and she estimated it to be well above freezing.

She tossed it up to excess heat leaking from the various machines that were still operating at the ship's centre. It would make sense. Eve must have been deep enough within the core of the *Eternity* that none of the cold from outside could waft in and sap away at the warmth like it did to her own body. She recalled what Eli had told her when they last explored the *Eternity*, something about the core still being active. *He was right,* she said to herself. *Whatever is powering this place is definitely something special.*

Her train of thought halted when her flashlight caught something just before her. Eve reached out and felt steel. Warm steel. It was the first barricade in her path since she began her descent, and a quick glance to her sides confirmed that it was a dead end. She felt around for a console, assuming it to be another bulkhead, but there was nothing. As far as she could tell, it was a wall.

'Great,' she tutted, 'now what?'

There was no response, though she did half-hope for a tell-tale whistle and green glow to illuminate to solve her conundrum.

Eve casted a glance back, her mind retrieving thoughts of Eli and Nisma. They must have found out she had left by now and were, no doubt, worried beyond belief. *They'd be looking for me,* she thought, picturing the sealed bulkhead at the other end of the tunnel. *They could cut me out.* Eve remembered the locator built into her jacket. *Surely the signal would reach this far. Or, at least, be visible from the bulkhead.*

She moved to turn around, but froze as the floor shook. Eve grabbed at the walls, finding some touchpoints in the form of pipes. A piercing light erupted from below as the floor split up the middle, mist pouring down the newly formed crevice like water down a ravine. Eve shrieked and leapt onto one side, gripping onto the wall. She watched in terror as the floor disappeared beneath her, vanishing underneath the walls and being replaced with such a magnificent light she could not stand to look into it for more than moments at a time.

After a short while the light dimmed slightly as something moved in between the source and Eve. She looked down and watched, through squinted eyes, as a small platform rose up out of the light and stopped level with an efficient clunk.

'Please proceed,' the familiar monotonous voice said, though its source eluded Eve due to the light.

She was apprehensive, but after a few test prods with her foot, she relented and lowered herself onto the platform. As soon as both of her feet were planted on the platform, it lurched and began its descent into the light.

It watched the child, whom it had determined to be called 'Eve' draw ever closer, obediently following each and every direction she was given. Sure, she took a bit of motivation through auditory and visual means and the sealing of the bulkhead ensured that the little human could only move in the direction it intended.

+*But, as far as mortal accomplices go, this little one is definitely a step above the rest in the control department.*+

Much unlike the other two, who were too wise and independent to be controlled easily. It paid special attention to their movements around the *Eternity* after they were able to reunite and inform each other of the situation.

+*A mistake on my behalf, to be sure,*+ it relented with a sigh that resonated out through the depths of the *Eternity's* innermost systems.

It had cursed itself for focussing so much on guiding the child on its path that it neglected to see the imminent reunion of Eli and Nisma. After their conversation they split ways, one delving deeper into the wreck towards Central Park and the other returning to their vehicle.

+*No doubt to use their radios and radar to their advantage in their search for the child,*+ it grumbled. It despised that radar and it could feel every pulse of radiation that emanated from it like a tsunami that penetrated through layers of steel and rock.

That made manipulation of travel routes difficult, but still easy enough to permit some level of alteration in its favour. It opened and closed doors, sealed airlocks, and lifted hydraulic walkways to slow Eli on his pursuit to Central Park. It knew it could not stop him; his knowledge of alternate routes and navigation was far too extensive for him to be fooled for long. But it could still delay him long enough for Eve to finish the task that it had laid out for her.

Thankfully, it did not have to wait long.

The child descended from the heavens atop her rickety platform. It had been such a long time since a human had entered its chamber. So long since it had the opportunity to behold such a creature without the need for external optics and cameras.

It could feel excitement bubble up from deep within it, manifesting as an electrical surge that zipped off down into the bowels of the *Eternity*. It received a warning that detailed several critical failures had occurred in the aquaponic systems contained in the aftmost agriculture district of sector thirty-two as a result of the overload. It cared little for such a trivial alert and dismissed it; the need for food production had long since been terminated along with the passengers who consumed it.

The platform reached ground level and melded in with the floor around it to make a perfectly flat surface. Eve was apprehensive, but eventually took the first step off the platform and towards the goal that had laid in wait for millennia.

Eve squinted with a hand cast against her forehead to block out as much of the light as possible. It took a few moments before her eyes could adjust to such an onslaught, blinking away the last of her night vision until she could see what was around her. She switched off her flashlight, its dull glow proving to be most inadequate for the present.

The room was massive, several hundred metres long, wide and tall. Great pillars, the same ones as those that held up the roof over Central Park, viced the floor and rooftop apart. Great lights lined the roof and illuminated everything within sight with a sanitary white light. The walls were the same steely material as the rest of the *Eternity,* but with a surprising lack of rust and decay. The air was also clear, the mist having dissipated and been replaced by a stale, but thankfully scentless atmosphere.

Great machines lined the walls, each several dozen metres in dimensions and connected to hundreds of cables, pipes and tubing. Some hummed with life, still performing whatever function they were designed to do all those years ago; others were idle, either rendered inoperable by time or their contribution proving to no longer be required. Between them were hundreds of desks, some with monitors and consoles and others with unrecognisable additions that sparked Eve's innate curiosity. Beside some of the desks were large, human-sized, vats filled with odd-looking fluids and solids that served to only fill Eve's mind with more questions than answers.

Eve's eyes salivated at the sight before her, her technophilic brain almost short-circuiting at the thought of so much undiscovered technology just waiting for her to discover. She found herself wandering around the room in a trance, bouncing from each great machine to the next, searching for secrets and anything she could pry off and stow in her bag for later examination. She even spared the time and patience to pause at a few desks, probing at the implements that sat atop their surfaces. But it was what lay at the end of the great room that proved to be most enticing.

At the head of the great room, several hundred metres away from where Eve had descended, stood an even bigger contraption. It grew from the floor and tapered out to the roof like the trunk of the trees in Central Park. At its base appeared to be a colossal bulkhead that sealed off whatever it contained from the rest of the universe. Untold thousands of cables and smaller devices branched off and funnelled into the walls, floor, roof or even the other large machines that cohabited the room alongside it. *Whatever it is,* Eve thought, feeling an otherworldly urge to approach the massive machine, *it's much more important than everything else here.*

Eve marched towards the machine, craning her neck upwards to take in its sheer mass. She did not stray from her path for long, only making the occasional stop to inspect elements and objects that managed to pull her attention away for a brief moment.

Before she knew it, she stood before the great bulkhead.

'Greetings, Citizen,' a familiar voice tweeted, pulling Eve's attention over to a console built in beside the bulkhead.

There was a small brass plaque screwed into the console above its screen that read: 'Ethereal Essence Transformer.'

'Ethereal Essence?' Eve asked.

'Unlock procedure initiated,' the console said before shutting off.

The floor shook, and Eve grabbed onto the console for balance. Beside her the great bulkheads began to shift, dragging their immense weight across the ground to create an opening just wide enough for Eve to slip through. She approached the opening cautiously, risking a glance at what was held within.

A small chamber lay before her, much smaller than she had anticipated, given the enormous exterior stature of the mechanism. It was dark, illuminated mainly by the light that flooded in through the newly formed opening that cast a reverse shadow across the steel floor. At the centre of the chamber was another source of light—a sturdy, transparent capsule that sat atop a chest-height podium of electronics and steel.

Inside the capsule was a small object roughly in the shape of a rectangular prism. It hovered at the epicentre of the capsule as if it were held in some form of stasis that defied gravity. An unusual aura emanated from it; a magnificent yet subtle cacophony of shade and hues that lazily transitioned from one end of the visual spectrum to the other in a cycle that emanated through time and space. It was hypnotising to Eve, and she found herself being drawn towards it in a trance.

She stopped just shy of the capsule, letting the colours dance across her face and chest as she beheld the object with gleeful wonder. It was a small rectangular tablet, no larger than the size of her palm, consisting of a brown, grainy material that Eve instantly correlated to the trunks of the trees in Central Park. A spiralling black and white twine fed out of a hole drilled into the top of the tablet and looped upon itself to form what Eve could only describe as a type of necklace. A humble black-and-white jewel was set into its centre, its crystalline insides swirling around in a constant battle for supremacy. None of these elements gave a clue as to the source of the splendid aura that surrounded the necklace, not a single viable source of emission.

'Welcome, Citizen,' the robotic voice mused from a nearby speaker system, the aura around the necklace flickering in unison with every syllable.

It watched Eve anxiously approach its form, the little human now being close enough to sense through its own ethereal means. Her slow pace was starting to ire on it, and it wanted to scream out at the child and order her to free it from its prison.

It was *so* close to freedom, so close to reaching the paramount of millennia of patient suffering. It missed home, and it wished with all its willpower to return to that place. But the rules of this reality had kept it shackled in its cell. It despised this place, the *'Eternity,'* as the builders' declared, a vessel that bound reality and the ethereal together in a matrimony that was supposed to spell the future of mankind. At least that was what they claimed.

For it, which had been intombed at the ship's heart from the very beginning and buried for the past ten thousand and eleven years, two hundred and seventy-three days, eight hours, twenty-two minutes and seventeen seconds, give or take a few due to the influence of temporal dilation, it had been agony.

When Eve had gotten close enough, it sent a signal out and activated the unlock sequence. A light hissing whisked out from the middle of the capsule epidermis as a clean rectangular incision was cut from its surface and dissolved into the air. Eve jumped a little and watched a light mist waft from the capsule and down to the ground, its ancient air now free to mingle with the putrid atmosphere of Concord. It waited for the child to reach in and take up its form, but she was apprehensive.

'Please proceed,' it said vocally, temporarily taking command of the local public address system.

It watched the child reach forward before she hesitated yet again.

+*Can't this damned thing take a hint?*+ it growled.

'Please take one,' the speaker system said. Its form glowed with each emphasised syllable it spoke, hoping to further establish a correlation between the words being said and the intent.

Eve's caution had eventually been whittled enough away for her to risk a grab at its form. Her fingers were soft, intimate, and gripped its form with a firm yet careful grasp. A light tug sent a shockwave of passion coursing through its entire form. There was some resistance from the mechanisms that held it in place, but they were no match for the strength of the child as a second tug tore it free of its torment.

A euphoric sensation rippled through it, an unbelievable feeling of relief and pain as the burden of supporting the systems of the *Eternity* were torn out piece by piece as every psychic thread that leashed it to the accursed ship was snapped free. In an instant its senses were blank, the network of instruments that served to give it critical information were disconnected for good. Its knowledge in the inner workings of every computer and system, regardless of their importance, vanished and freed up untold quantities of thought-power that could be utilised for more productive issues.

With its thoughts cleared up, it could now set its attention to phase two of its plan. The first step being escaping the *Eternity* alive. *+I do not wish for my prison to become my tomb. Let's hope this little one copes well under pressure.+*

'Eve? Eve?!' Eli shouted out as he ran, tearing through the corridors at break-neck speed. His voice, remixed with the rapid beat of his boots on the steel floor, reverberated out into the labyrinth.

He hoped that if he had kicked up enough of a ruckus, Eve would reveal herself—or at least call back to him. But, so far, he had no such luck, and he continued on his path towards Central Park where Eve's last known location was. He called out again and again, but there was still no response. His mind began to wander and contemplate what his daughter was up to. What if she's been injured? Or gotten lost? *She could be dead! Like everyone else!* He shook his head, the thoughts threatening to send his emotional state down a steep drop.

'No,' he growled, shoving the dreadful thoughts of the past and the speculative present out of his mind. 'She's at Central Park. Probably looking at the trees or something.'

He slowed his pace a little, a sudden intersection appearing in his shaky flashlight beam, and took the right path. Sweat drenched his face and soaked his jackets, a result of the strenuous activity and the gradually rising temperature. He wiped at his brow with his sleeve only for another wave of perspiration to replace it a few seconds later. His goggles were fogged, and his mask stuck to his face like a leech, but he paid little heed to such distractions.

Eli cursed under his breath at his daughter's stupidity. *Why did you leave? Why go out here on your own? You're smarter than that, Eve!* He wondered for a moment, and it clicked in his head. *That robot! That damned robot! She's out here looking for parts for it! Dammit, Eve.* He could not help but agree with Nisma's sentiments on letting their daughter explore the *Eternity. She's right. We should not be doing something so stupid at a time like this. I shouldn't have put the idea of exploring this place in Eve's head just to spite her.*

A rustling in his ear made him pause his thought-train. 'Eve?' he asked into his radio.

'It's me, Eli,' Nisma's voice responded, audibly exhausted. 'I just got back.'

'Can you raise her? I'm not getting anything.'

Eli had tried raising Eve's radio non-stop since he and Nisma had met up, the need for secrecy now redundant.

Unfortunately, there had been no responses from their daughter.

There were a few moments of silence during which Eli assumed Nisma was attempting to do the same and he hoped that the exponentially more powerful radios aboard the Rover might have a better chance at yielding an answer. During this time, he had to slow and squeeze himself through a half-stuck bulkhead before picking back up to full speed.

'Negative,' Nisma eventually confirmed, irritable. 'Either she's turned it *off* or is in a place where the signal can't reach.'

Eli bit back a retort to Nisma's obvious reference to their last visit to the *Eternity*. *Now's not the time, Nis*, he said in his head.

'You know where she is, though?' he asked instead, putting the argument behind for the time being.

'She's at Central Park... Wait. What?'

'Nis, what is it?'

Her answer did not fill him with confidence. 'Her locator is returning a grid reference three hundred metres *below* the greenery level of the park.'

Eli poured his mind over the layout of Central Park, something he had memorised long before the *Eternity's* arrival over Concord, but could not think of any feasible means as to how Eve could have reached such a location. 'There's no pitfalls that deep in Central Park, and all the doorways were deadlocked last I checked.'

'Well, she got there *somehow*,' Nisma spat.

Eli had quickly grown tired of Nisma's prods and readied a response, but was cut short by a sudden tremor beneath him. 'What the—?'

The ground lurched up under him as a powerful thrust heaved from deep within the *Eternity* and slammed back down. Eli yelped as he landed hard on his stomach, barely managing to get his arms in a position to brace against the rough landing. He groaned as sharp pains rippled all over his body where he made contact with the metal floor. *Did the whole damn ship just leap up?*

'Eli? What's happening?' Nisma asked with worry, her toxic tone dissipating in an instant.

Eli tried to rise to his feet, but several smaller aftershocks made the act an endeavour in balance. He managed to use a stray pipeline protruding from the wall to heave himself up. 'The ship just shook,' he answered, wincing as he touched a soft spot on his shin. 'Any tectonic activity?'

He could hear rapid typing in his ear as Nisma worked to pull up a reading. 'Richter scale shows nothing,' she said, each word filled with intent as she undoubtedly scanned the data with machine efficiency. 'Wait, I'm getting something… Seismic activity. Originating from…*within* the *Eternity*!'

'Within?!' Eli repeated, not believing her words.

'Within,' Nisma confirmed followed by more typing. 'I'm also reading radiation spikes all across the wreck. Something's happening to the *Eternity*!'

'Shit,' Eli swore, taking off at full pelt once again, 'I'm nearly at Central Park.'

'Hurry, Eli!'

'That's what I'm doing!'

Eli must have reached Central Park in record time, bursting out onto one of the uppermost walkways that overlooked the centrepiece of the *Eternity* in a fit of splutters and gasps. He wasted no time, immediately jogging up to the balustrade and peering down into the spectacle of wavering luminescent lamps and rustling trees. His eyes could not pick up any hint of Eve, body or flashlight, and there was no indication of a cave-in to assist him in learning how she managed to delve so deep into the steel.

'Where's she at, Nis?' he radioed, taking off with one hand on the railing and his head peering it over at the abyss.

'Her locator shows her coming up to the surface in a hurry,' Nisma answered. 'Whatever's happening has certainly scared her.'

'Roger, I'll—' Eli started before being cut off by an ear-splitting snap.

Across the park, a colossal section of the roof tore free of its frame. It fell for a few seconds in total silence, its matte steel form being illuminated gold by the sunlamps beneath it and silver by Concord Minor above it. Eli was awestruck by it and watched as it plummeted to the ground, landing with a great crash that flattened a segment of Central Park the size of a football field and shook the vessel to its foundations.

The deafening smash tore Eli from his trance. 'The ship's tearing itself apart!'

'You're almost there, Eli. Eve's nearly at the surface, just keep going down!'

'Right.'

Eli took off for the nearest descending staircase, leaping down several steps at a time before repeating the process down the next set all the while keeping his eyes peeled out over the park beneath him.

As he ran, his eyes picked up strange glimpses of figures below and he could have sworn he saw vague shadows of the couples who used to walk along the marbled paths between the trees and of the families who sat on the grass, feeling every individual blade between their fingers and the warmth of the lamps on their faces. They were unusually calm and carefree, the spectres of those who had spent their entire lives encapsulated in the *Eternity* with their eyes set on the future. *The true horrors of Concord were not even given a passing thought,* he internally grimaced. *If only we knew what was about to happen. All those untold billions who spent their lives sealed in this metal chamber, only for it to become both their crib and casket.*

He sighed as he ran through all the memories that were born in that place. His family. His friends. His life before the crash. Everything. He missed it all so much and, while he knew they were no longer with him, in a way, he felt closer to them every time he strode through those dark corridors, those same corridors that he, too, had walked his entire life. To him, *Eternity* was home, it was all he knew, and to see it all fall apart before him made a tear break from his eye.

Halfway down the second to last set, another great tremor shook the ship and tore Eli from his thoughts. He gripped onto the handrails, and his footing was kicked loose by the quake. The staircases and walkways waved in the air and ancient, Rain-weakened, mountings flexed under their immense weight. This proved to be the death knell for one segment of walkway above Eli.

With a horrific snap the several tonnes of steel broke free and cascaded down onto the staircase Eli was bracing on. It smashed into the lower portion of the staircase, tearing it free from its lower mounting and shaking the staircase like a wooden plank before vanishing below. Eli was thrown skywards with a yelp, but he held onto the railing with all his strength. He landed hard, feeling several hard knocks in his torso as he collided with the steps. A searing pain swiftly followed, filling his entire abdomen with unbelievable torment.

'Eli?!' Nisma shouted in his ear in a panic. 'What's happening?!'

Eli groaned, trying to rise to his feet, but the staircase he was sprawled on was not finished as its upper mountings, now straining under the increased pressure, also tore free. Eli could do little else, but hold on as best he could as he plummeted along with the staircase down into the dark, screaming all the way.

'Eli? Eli, are you okay?!' Nisma's desperate calls echoed as he fell. 'Eli?!'

CHAPTER SIX

The ground shook violently as if an earthquake was tearing up the ground around Eve. She glanced back to see the bulkhead grinding closed.

'No!' she shrieked, whipping around and sprinting as fast as she could for the rapidly narrowing exit. She made it to the bulkhead and slid through, sucking her gut in as it closed in around her. A desperate leap to the side cleared Eve of the bulkhead a split second before it sealed shut. She landed heavy on her shoulder and winced as she rose to her feet. A few prods with her opposite hand yielded a searing response. *Hope it's not broken.*

Explosions inundated the great room as fuse boxes blew and overloaded machinery detonated. Sparks showered from torn cables, and noxious fluids flooded from burst piping and cracked capsules.

'Warning. Critical power surge,' the public service announcement system declared. 'All systems failing.'

'Shit,' Eve swore, looking around at the scene that was unfurling before her. She wanted to run, but had no idea of where to go.

'Please don't keep the elevator waiting,' the speaker system tutted, the necklace in Eve's hand glowing with each syllable.

Eve shot a confused glance at the necklace before it clicked in her head. *The platform!*

She took off towards the platform, its shape beginning to rise up out of the floor and start its journey to the heavens. Pocketing the necklace, Eve charged through spark showers and torrents of liquid, using her bag to cover her exposed head. A cascade of toppling cables that had blown free of their housings in one of the great machines forced Eve to alter her route, their collision with the floor sending shards of steel and insulation flying in all directions. Eve felt a sharp pain in her side as one such projectile punctured her clothes and bit into her flesh. She could feel the spreading warmth of blood immediately after. She winced, but pushed through the pain, her adrenaline already dulling its effects and putting her into a trance focussed on reaching the platform no matter what.

The lights shimmered, some of the bulbs blowing out to add their own sparks and debris to the cacophony. Eve now found herself running through patches of light and dark— piercing brightness and eternal shadows. It made navigation of the rapidly decaying scene before her difficult. Not aided at all by her mask which clung to her face and her hair that was plastered to her foggy goggles. Sweat inundated her filter to the point where every breath included a healthy dose of salty water. She considered changing it, but knew she was in a situation that demanded speed, and she was *so* close to making it. *I can take a little bit of bad air.*

The platform was fifty metres away, but it was reaching a height that Eve questioned she climbed up to. She kicked into her highest gear and powered her legs as quickly as they could go. Her breathing was strained, the waterlogged filter depriving her of more oxygen with each passing second.

She could feel her lungs scream for air, her heart thump in her chest and adrenaline course through her ears. Her vision grew blurry, and her head swayed a bit. *No! Not this time!* Eve pushed away the unsteadiness as best she could, clearing up her head enough for her to realise she would need to jump to make it onto the platform.

With every ounce of strength, she leapt free of the ground. She flew in the air for several metres before she landed with a heavy thud against the side of the platform. Eve felt sick to her stomach as the impact crushed her ribcage, but she managed to grasp onto the platform with slippery gloved hands. She grunted and groaned, her arms and shoulders straining under the stress of such an awkward position. Her legs wagged from side to side as she tried in vain to haul herself up. She cast a quick glance down to see that the platform was now well above the ground—a fall that would result in a severe injury at the least.

Mustering up the last of her strength, Eve dragged herself up and onto the level platform, slumping down to look at the chaos below. She sighed, thankful to have escaped with her life, and watched the room beneath her tear itself apart in a spectacle of destruction.

She soon found herself back in the tunnel, and she held her breath for as long as she could, dreading the inevitable inhalation of the nauseating mist. Her olfactory senses must have developed a minute tolerance to the stench, but it did little to keep her stomach from turning over.

Tremors tore through the dark tunnel, disturbing the mist and rattling Eve's very bones. Her vision was poor, the mist eating up all of her flashlight's beam after a few metres. For the most part, she managed to remain upright and keep her heading, but every so often, her footing would slip the tiniest bit and result in a desperate scramble for balance. Her head and shoulders ached from the numerous collisions she made with the rough industrial tunnel walls, and Eve could feel a welling warmth seep down the side of her face where her Mark had opened up. It did not bother Eve; she knew she was close to the bulkhead that led out into Central Park.

The mist had begun to thin, and her radio caught the occasional snippet of chatter between Eli and Nisma. Although the signal was still too choppy for Eve to accurately decipher what was being said, she could tell from their panicked tones that her absence had certainly been noticed and they were now coordinating a search operation of some kind.

Eve cursed her sudden rebellious urge to go out on her own. She had hoped her unauthorised excursion would have gone unnoticed until she returned with Spud's components in hand. Now her parents were worried beyond belief and were likely scouring the *Eternity* as it was falling apart just to find her. She pushed the thoughts out of her head for the moment. *I still gotta get out of* here *first.*

Before Eve knew it, a familiar staircase emerged from the fog before her and ascended up to her exit. She covered the steps in quick succession and found herself before the bulkhead once again. Eve took in deep breaths and savoured the air, now free of the putrid mist. Her relief was short lived, and she turned her attention to the colossal slab of steel before her.

'No console. No panels. Nothing,' she tutted to herself, feeling around the bulkhead for even a fleeting hint of how to open it.

As she pondered how to tackle the situation, a slow-growing heat in her pants quickly became unbearably hot. Eve yelped and dug through her pockets, fishing out the necklace. It glowed with such intensity that she had to avert her eyes from it. The bulkhead grinded open, revealing the familiar sight of Central Park beyond. Eve was dumbstruck, taking her first steps through and back into the open world.

She glanced at the necklace quizzically. 'Did *you* do this?'

The necklace gave no answer, and Eve cursed herself for thinking that a clothing accessory could speak.

But it did *do something,* she thought before a burst of static in her ear drew her attention away from the necklace.

'Eli?!' a desperate Nisma hollered out across the radio waves. 'Eli, respond!'

'Mom?' Eve said into her piece, pocketing the necklace for safe keeping.

'Eve?! Is that you?' Nisma asked, her voice thick with relief. 'Are you okay?'

Her mother's tone sent ripples of guilt throughout Eve; she did not know she had made them *that* anxious with her absence. Eve swallowed, half choking on her words. 'I'm okay, Mom.'

'Good. Good,' Nisma said with a sigh. 'Your locator says you're in Central Park, correct?'

Eve grunted in confirmation.

'Okay,' Nisma started, giving weight to her static-ridden voice. 'Eli—your father isn't responding to my hails. He's close by. I need you to find him and see if he's okay. You got that?'

Eve nodded, taken aback by the severity of the situation she now found herself in. 'Okay.'

'Good girl,' Nisma acknowledged, followed by rapid tapping. 'I'll guide you on to him. And be quick; I don't think the ship will stay together for much longer.'

As if to emphasise her point, a loud crash shook Central Park to its core as hundreds of tonnes of metal smashed into the ground in a distant corner of the park. Eve struggled to keep her footing, and she feared the ground would disappear beneath her. Her vision blurred, and her ears squealed as the cacophony of chaos rattled inside her head. A sudden bout of nausea, accompanied by a few nasty gags, threatened to upheave Eve's last meal, but she fought it back down.

'He's a few hundred metres to the north,' Nisma said, more a niggling drone than a human voice over the auditory feedback in Eve's ear. 'If you're looking in towards the park, it'll be on your right. Go!'

Eve took off, her legs seizing control from her mind. It was a few moments until her vision and thoughts cleared up enough for her to properly understand what she was doing, her brain finally collecting all of the marbles it had dropped.

'You got that, Eve?' Nisma's voice inquired sternly in Eve's ear.

'I got it, Mom!' Eve shouted back, her ringing ears altering her perception of volume.

She ran alongside the outer wall of the park, keeping an eye out for any sign of her father while remaining in relative safety from the downpour of metal.

As she went Eve found herself casting her eyes over the carnage that was unfurling around her. Several great segments of the roof and walkways had already broken free and crushed entire groves of the magnificent trees and their supporting infrastructure, piling up on top of themselves in ever-growing mounds of twisted metal. Some had landed with enough weight and force to tear through the reinforced floor and cascade down through to the lower levels of the ship to wreak further havoc. Eve wondered if she could catch a glimpse of the breathtaking room and the many machines it contained at the bottom of one of the deep chasms, but she dared not risk a look.

The only sections of the park that remained stoic in the face of such destruction were the towering pillars that rose up from the depths of the lower levels and pierced up into the exposed sky where the roofing around them had fallen away. They stood there, ever vigilant amongst the untold thousands of stars that sprinkled what meagre rays of light they could manage to cross such vast distances from their origin. This was matched in harmony with the rocking beams of warm artificial light from the few sunlamps that remained operational.

'You're nearly there, Eve,' Nisma's voice whined in her ear. 'Just twenty metres.'

Eve slowed down and casted her flashlight side to side across the ground, scanning for any signs of Eli. 'Dad?!' she called out, keeping up her search pattern as she walked. 'Dad?!'

A pang of guilt washed over her again. *Please be okay. I'm so sorry. Just please be okay. It's all my fault.* An anomalous form on the ground made Eve's heart skip a beat, and she aimed her flashlight onto it. But, much to her disappointment, it was merely a length of rebar that formed part of a larger mass of twisted debris.

'You're right on top of him, Eve. Do you see him?'

Eve looked around her, finding nothing but scrap. *There's only rubble here*, she thought before it clicked in her head. *On top…*

Her heart dropped in her chest. 'No,' she grumbled, casting her eyes over the pile and hoping with all her soul that it was not true, 'No, no, no, no—Dad, no!'

'Eve?' Nisma asked, thick with concern.

Eve ignored her. She dropped to her knees and tore through the wreckage, prying up any piece of twisted serrated metal she could lift and throwing it aside.

'Daddy, please, no!' she begged, tears rapidly filled her goggles and snot flooded her mask. Her gloves and sleeves were torn to shreds in quick succession, rapidly replaced by growing swells of blood that stained her hands a slick crimson. Eve did not stop, her desperation urging her to push onwards regardless of injury. 'I'm sorry! I'm sorry, Daddy!' she cried, her words turning into deranged bumbling.

'Eve? That you?' a husky voice said from beneath the rubble.

'Dad?!' Eve shrieked, casting her flashlight down every gap in the debris she could find. The light caught a brief glimpse of her father's jacket deep within a small opening by her feet. Eve dropped to her stomach and cast her flashlight in.

Eli lay before her, having found refuge in a small cavern created by the wreckage as it landed. Her flashlight glinted on his face, making him stir. He strained to tilt his head in Eve's direction, azure eyes regarding her with a squint over his goggles that had fallen down his face. His blond hair was stained brown with dried blood.

'It *is* you,' he smiled. His breathing was ragged, and a shrill hissing could be heard from his mask where several ruptures had broken the airtight seal.

'Your mask!' Eve pointed out, holding back tears.

'I know. I know.' Eli nodded, feeling at the torn sections of his mask. 'Come on. Get me out of here.' He held out a hand for Eve to grab.

Eve took it up and immediately noticed some irregularities in its shape. It was definitely broken in several areas. The sight was familiar, and it made her hesitate.

'Let's go, Eve,' Eli encouraged, giving her hand a shake.

Eve nodded, putting the uncomfortable thoughts away for the moment. She took up a braced position and gave one almighty tug followed by another. Eli groaned as he was slowly extracted from the rubble one violent yank at a time. Every grunt of pain from her father made Eve feel sick to her stomach, something further emphasised by the unhealthy clicks and clacks that cricked from his body. She closed her eyes and tried to block out the sounds, but it did no good.

'Okay, that's good,' Eli mumbled, unusually calm considering the situation he was in.

Eve dropped his hand carefully and straightened up. The sight was not pretty. Eli's clothing was in tatters, flashlight destroyed and his backpack was ruined. Countless cuts and bruises covered his body, and several fingers were crumpled or missing all together. Most horrifying, however, was the state of his right leg, which was disfigured and crushed beyond recognition. Blood poured out from morbid lacerations peaked by segments of shattered bone and sinew.

'Oh, no. Daddy, you're—' Eve started before gagging. She averted her eyes, emotions threatening to take over. Her knees wobbled, though she could not tell if it was the frequent tremors from the ground or her adrenaline surpassing critical levels. A firm hand viced around Eve's arm and pulled her to her knees. Eve spun her head around to see Eli glaring directly at her.

'Eve. I *need* you to calm down and listen *very* carefully,' he growled between coughs. 'There should still be some tape in my bag. Get it out.'

Eve swallowed and nodded in acknowledgment. She leant over her father and dug through the remnants of his bag.

A sudden quake rocked the ground and sent another section of the roof toppling to the ground in a crash.

'Hurry!' Eli shouted, bordering on anger.

His tone made Eve jump in surprise. She sniffled and held back more tears as she expedited her search, quickly finding the familiar touch of a tape roll and reeling it in. Her fingers fumbled with the roll for a few seconds until she managed to tear off a length. She handed it to Eli, who took it up with some difficulty and fastened it to his mask, sealing a rupture. They repeated this several more times until Eli held out a hand to stop Eve. He purged the mask and took in a few deep breaths. Eve watched the mask's rubberised form stretch and relax in response.

'Okay,' he said with a raspy cough. 'Eve? You good?'

Eve nodded silently; her whole body was red hot in fear.

Eli shifted with a pained grunt, and his eyes locked on his right leg. 'Eve, I need you to take your belt off.'

His request took a second to register in Eve's brain, her mind already inundated with thousands of thoughts and heart-racing chemicals. 'B-belt?' she bumbled eventually, glancing down at her waist.

Eli nodded. 'Yes, take it off.'

Eve was hesitant, but eventually obliged. She straightened up and parted her jackets. With unsteady hands she unbuckled her belt and extracted it out of the loops. For a moment she feared her pants would fall down, but they remained stalwart in place. She held it out to Eli like a leathery serpent, unsure of what to do next.

'Now, loop it around my leg,' Eli instructed, pointing at his mangled limb. 'As if you were putting it on, and make it *super* tight.'

'Okay.' Eve nodded, taking a knee beside Eli's mangled leg.

She threaded the belt underneath, taking note to lift the mutilated limb as carefully as possible, but a few grunts from her father made her shudder in terror. Eve reached over the leg and extracted the end of the belt, noticing a healthy layer of lubricant had been collected with it during its journey underneath. She pulled her hand away and examined the substance in her flashlight. It was thick and crimson and oozed down into every crack and crevice on her hands. She could feel it seep through the cuts in her gloves and loosen her fingers with their unsettling warmth and oily consistency. Tears started to roll down her face; she was at the brink of breaking down.

'I *need* you to focus, Eve,' Eli growled, grabbing her jacket and yanking her head down to his eye level. 'Now's not the time to sob!'

Eve nodded and sniffled. She instinctively wiped at her eyes, but was met by her goggles instead. Eli released his grasp and Eve straightened back up, her attention returning to the task at hand.

She readied to tighten the belt, but Eli interjected, 'A bit higher, as close to my hips as possible.'

Eve nodded and shimmied the belt as high as she could get it up the leg, averting her eyes as she crossed a chunk of protruding bone. More blood covered her hands and belt, making her grip slippery.

'Make sure you do it really tight,' Eli said, taking a few deep breaths.

Eve nodded and threaded the belt through the buckle. After getting a nod of approval from Eli, she pulled it tight. The belt clenched around Eli's thigh, and he groaned through gritted teeth.

'Sorry!' Eve spluttered, letting go of the belt.

'No!' Eli shouted. 'It *needs* to be tight, Eve! For fucks sake!'

Eve fumbled with the belt end before giving another pull, much harder this time.

'Fuck me!' Eli winced.

Blood spurted from the wound as fractured bones shifted under the pressure, painting Eve's mask and goggles. She shuddered and tried in vain to wipe it off with her sleeve, but her efforts only served to smudge and spread it around. *Why won't it come off?!* A steadying hand from Eli stopped her bickering and helped guide the belt into place in the buckle.

'Okay,' Eli sighed. 'Help me up.' He grunted as he shuffled into a seated position, keeping his injured leg straight, and held out his arm as an invitation.

Eve took the hint and scampered to his side, bracing his arm over her shoulders.

'Ready?' Eli asked, coy.

Eve wriggled under his arm, taking up a squat. 'Y-yeah.'

'One. Two. Three.'

Eve lifted with all her might, feeling the colossal weight of her father bear down upon her back and legs. For a moment she thought she was going to fold like a book, but the weight eased off once Eli got high enough to lend some assistance with his ambulatory leg. A few seconds of wobbling heralded the rest of their ascension, Eli leaning heavily on his daughter

like a crutch, before they carefully navigated the debris back down to the ground.

'You hearing that, Eve?' Eli pointed out, tapping at his ear. 'My radio's busted, but I think Nis is trying to talk to you.'

'Oh,' Eve mumbled. She was so tunnel visioned that she failed to notice her mother speaking in her ear.

'What was that, Mom?'

'*Don't* ignore me again, Eve,' Nisma spat before lightening her tone. 'Is your father okay? You find him?'

Eve grumbled at her mother's scolding, but left it as an internal gripe. 'He's hurt really bad. But we can walk.'

'Excellent,' Nisma said followed by keyboard tapping.

Her response struck Eve as unusually impartial given the situation.

'I don't know what's happening with the ship, Eve,' Nisma continued, 'but the fail-safes keeping its coolant reserves steady have been disabled. You need to get out of there now.'

'What's she saying?' Eli interjected.

'She says we need to get out now,' Eve relayed.

'Tell me something I *don't* know,' he tutted, glancing around at the destruction around them.

Eve figured he was looking for a way out to the Rover, but with the ship rapidly disintegrating around them, viable exit routes were becoming scarcer by the second. She felt a growing warmth in her pocket yet again, and she fished out the necklace. It gave off the same hypnotising aura it had before and Eve had to look away slightly to protect her eyes.

'What the hell is that?' Eli asked, having noticed the strange lights coming from Eve's hand.

The ground shook as metal grinded on metal. Eve and Eli looked skywards for falling debris, but nothing came. Instead, a large section of the wall nearby had begun to part ways, revealing a wide corridor that vanished off in the dark.

Its job done for now, the necklace dimmed and returned to its slumber. Eve regarded it with curiosity, but was shaken back to reality as Eli yanked her flashlight from its mount. He waved the light down the corridor.

'I know this tunnel!' he exclaimed, waving the torch over an ancient hieroglyph scrawled on one of the tunnel's walls. 'There's a quick way out through here! Tell your mother to be ready with the Rover by the slides.'

'O-okay,' Eve said, her father's use of the term dumbfounding her.

She fumbled with the radio. 'Mom?'

Nisma's response was quick. 'Yes?'

'Daddy says to be ready by the slides.'

Her next response was not particularly enthusiastic. 'Okay. Roger.'

'What'd she say?' Eli inquired in a manner that hinted he already knew Eve's answer.'

Eve glanced at him with a raised eyebrow. 'She said "okay," but she didn't sound too happy.'

Eli chuckled, but said nothing more that pertained to the subject. 'All right, let's get a move on.'

Eve nodded and they took off towards the bulkhead. As they passed through the threshold between the corridor and the park, she shot a fleeting glance back. She watched the trees sway and shake under their rocking lamp shades as more tremors ripped through the ship. Many of the stalwart beings had already been felled by the violent quakes or crushed by the debris that continued to fall from the sky above. A pang of sadness washed over her as the last tree disappeared from her sight and was swallowed up by the dark of the corridor.

It was not long before they came up to what Eli had coined the 'slides,' though Eve immediately recognised their true purpose as a form of exhaust expulsion system, probably used to escape the gravitational pull of Earth. They were a pair of massive pipes that passed through an abandoned warehouse diagonally from roof to ground level with no regard for ergonomics. One of the pipes had a rough human-sized opening cut into it and evidence of a blowtorch or buzz saw exacting their wrath on the exposed metal around its edges.

Eve helped her father up to the opening, and he peered through. 'Ask your mother if she's in position.'

'Are you in position?' Eve relayed.

'Yes, but I don't think that—' Nisma's response was cut short by the largest tremor yet.

Eve and Eli braced as best they could as the ship shuddered under the stress. Rebars and doorways collapsed. Pipelines burst, spraying gases and liquids all over. A putrid stench of expired lubricants melted through Eve's filters and invaded her nose. She grimaced, but was thankful that it was nowhere near as bad as the mists.

'It's time to go,' Eli announced, taking hold of Eve and shoving her into the opening.

Eve yelped as he thrusted her inside, landing hard on her back. Before she could recover, she felt friction disappear and her body enter motion. She looked back and saw the opening vanish in the distance. Darkness quickly engulfed her and she slid about uncontrollably with no means of stopping. She was terrified, but deep down, she could not help but feel a creeping sense of enjoyment from the ride. It ended as quickly as it began, and Eve was shot out of the pipe and entered freefall. She screamed as the outside world materialised before her, and her arms flailed for something to grab onto. She landed in a heap on something metallic, sliding to a halt by a stack of antennae. It took her a moment to realise that she had landed on the roof of the Rover. She looked up in time to see Eli plummet from the pipe opening and land hard beside her.

'Fuck,' he groaned and gripped at his leg before rolling over and slamming a fist into the roof three times.

The Rover lurched and rolled off from the *Eternity* as fast as it could, kicking up mounds of dirt and rocks as it went.

Eve glanced at Eli, his form now visible in the light of Concord Minor, as he sat up and leaned back against an antenna. It groaned in response, but held his weight.

He sighed, flipped the flashlight off and held it out to Eve. 'Here.'

Eve nodded and took her flashlight back, returning it to its mount. She swallowed. She had caught a glimpse of his injured leg before he'd killed the light. It made her heart sink.

'Daddy. I—' she started, but caught a lump in her throat. She was already shivering, the stark change in temperature already showing the deficiencies of her tattered clothing.

Eli motioned for her to come by his side. 'It's all right, Eevee,' he said calmly. 'All that matters is you're safe.'

His tone helped appease Eve's grief a little, and she accepted his invitation. She crawled up to his uninjured side and cuddled up against him, burying her face in his chest. She wept quietly, not bothering to empty her goggles as they slowly filled with her tears. Eli lowered his arm over her and took up one of her hands with his to help sooth her.

'Radiation spike,' Nisma's voice announced over Eve's radio. 'Brace yourselves.'

Eve raised her head, but Eli pressed her back down. 'Better cover your eyes for this.'

Eve obeyed, but still managed to peek an eye out from behind her father's hand. She watched the *Eternity*, its colossal form growing ever smaller as the Rover carried them away. There was a small flash, silent. Then a great blinding light that consumed the *Eternity* whole. Eve averted her eyes for a moment, but looked back as soon as the light dimmed. There was nothing; only raining debris and the occasional spot fire across the ground.

CHAPTER SEVEN

Chunks of flaming metal plummeted from the sky and crashed into the tired earth and gravel around them, kicking up mountains of debris in a terrifying spectacle of fire and rock. Eve was used to the meteor showers that frequently rained down on Concord from the shattered remains of Minor, but never had she been caught out in the open in the midst of one. It would have been beyond horrifying had she not been so exhausted and emotionally drained.

The Rover jumped and bounced. Antennae snapped free, and aged components were shorn off. Eve rode out with her father in the cold for as long as they could, feeding off of each other's warmth, before they eventually descended onto one of the many ramshackle gangplanks that circumvented the exterior of the Rover and into the ancillary airlock that granted access to the roof. It was a rough ride, and the gangplanks lacked any form of proper railing or structural integrity after a decade on Concord, which made their traversal tenuous at best, but Eve and Eli managed to slip inside without further incident.

Once inside Eli headed straight for the medbay, leaning heavily against his daughter-crutch. Eve's knees wobbled under his weight and the violent travel, but she soldiered on. She opened the medbay door, and they limped inside. Eli groaned as he laid down onto the bed, immediately staining the sanitary bedspreads crimson. He peeled off his mask and goggles and tossed them aside with a sigh, revealing a healthy cut along his cheek that correlated with one of the taped-up splits in his mask.

Eve removed her own protective gear, letting them hang loosely around her neck, and she immediately got to work. She ripped open drawers and cabinets to retrieve bandages, padding and ointments, all of which were out of date, but they were all she could work with. She was well versed in basic first aid and could readily apply bandaging to the minor lacerations. But the serious cuts, and especially the leg, were far beyond her ability. Regardless, she applied the bandages with slick efficiency, wincing at every pained grunt that drifted from Eli's mouth.

Not long after, the Rover grinded to a halt and powered down. The medbay door opened, and Nisma marched in, immediately relieving Eve with a stern push to the side. Eve watched meekly from the side for a few moments as Nisma examined and then promptly dismantled all of her work with a disgusted tut. Her heart sank with every soiled bandage, every wasted drop of disinfectant and every piece of strapping used to hold everything together that was thrown to the ground. Eve dared to risk a glance at her mother's face, but could only feel an overwhelming sense of anger that pushed her eyes back to the ground. She took the hint and slinked out into the common room, closing the door behind her and relegating herself to her bedroom.

Eve had lost track of how long had passed. It felt like a dream, but she could not remember closing her eyes for any longer than a moment, let alone fall asleep. *Maybe this was all a dream?* she had pondered in one grasping moment. *Maybe soon I'll wake up and this'll all be over and everything will be back to normal?* She shook the thought away as quickly as it had manifested. *This isn't a dream. It's a nightmare.* Her stomach would occasionally grumble in protest, but Eve would ignore its primal demands for sustenance. She had long since discarded her mask, goggles and bloody jackets and left them in a pile atop her bed. Her black hair was matted and oily, her face covered in grit and grime streaked with tear marks—the result of several breakdowns during her isolation.

The entire Rover was quiet, unusually so. Eve had initially strained to listen in on what would have been occurring in the room beside her own, but to no avail. The walls of the medbay, unlike the rest of the Rover, were designed to contain sound and the silence ate away at her insides as an ever-growing muteness that pressed down upon her from all sides like the suffocating black of the eternal night outside. It weighed down on her shoulders and kept her planted firmly in her seat with her arms at her workbench.

Only the occasional clink from the Rover or the muffled thud that echoed into the cave as yet another piece of the *Eternity* met its final resting place in the ground outside broke the monotony. It gave Eve a brief moment of change from the norm, but the quiet could only be belated for so long before it returned and, in a way, she almost craved the loud arguments that heralded the start of this escapade to the *Eternity*.

At least that way, she could derive some sense of familiarity. But this, the quiet that forced her ears to manufacture white noise and to leave her all alone with her thoughts and grievances...

It was the worst she had ever felt.

Spud's head rocked about soothingly in Eve's grasp. She was locked in a staring contest with his inactive optics, her reflection meeting her gaze just as vehemently. She had tried to get some work done on him to take her mind off things, but her brain drew a blank and her hands remained unproductive, preferring to idly fiddle with various tools and components instead.

A door opened outside, and Eve immediately straightened up. It was the first sign of any activity outside of her room in what must have been hours. Footsteps pattered up to the exterior of her door. They were heavy, purposeful. Eve deduced them to be the steps of her mother.

The door slid open, and on the other side stood Nisma. She was a mess; her forearms and rolled-up sleeves were stained crimson, her olive skin worn and exhausted from hours of endless work and her curly black hair a mess from lack of care. Her eyes were shrouded in a shadow cast by her brow.

Her words were blunt: 'Your father wants to see you. You have a few minutes.' She stepped to the side as an invitation to Eve to pass through.

Eve was apprehensive. She was not sure if she could bear to see her father at that moment. The injuries he had suffered, the pain he was in. She looked up to her mother, who had a firm look on her face that told Eve that it was not a matter for debate. Eve nodded meekly, carefully set Spud's head down on the workbench and shuffled out into the common room. Nisma closed the door behind her and marched straight for the medbay door. She ushered Eve to come close, and she did. With a press of the console, the medbay door opened, and Eve instantly caught a lump in her throat.

Eli lay on his back on the bed. Large portions of his body were wrapped in bandaging and numerous tubes ran from himself to either a machine or one of the drips that were suspended from the roof above him. A clear mask held an airtight seal to his face, feeding oxygen and likely other chemicals directly to his damaged respiratory system.

His azure eyes lit up at the sight of Eve. 'Hey, Eevee.' He waved with a smile.

A firm push from behind made Eve's legs finally turn over. She approached her father warily. The floor was littered with bloody bandages and rubbish. She tried to avoid stepping on them, and every crunch and squish sent shivers up her spine. As she drew near, she could feel a growing sadness in her heart that peaked at breaking point as she stopped by her father's bedside. Tears threatened to burst free, but she managed to hold them at bay.

Eli must have noticed her sorry state. 'Nothing to worry about here, Eevee.' He chuckled in a manner that sounded too much like a coughing bout for Eve's liking. 'In a few cycles it'll be business as usual.'

Eve casted her eyes down to his legs and immediately noticed that his right leg was considerably shorter than his left. 'Wh-what happened to your—'

'There was too much trauma,' Nisma explained frankly. 'I couldn't save the leg.'

That proved to be the final straw for Eve. 'Daddy…' she whimpered, the first tear breaking through, 'I'm so sorry!' She dropped to her knees and buried her face into the bed beside Eli. Tears poured from her eyes and drenched the bloody bedspreads. She spluttered and spat, taking desperate gasps for air in between bouts of emotional turmoil.

Eli was aback, but he was quick to rest a comforting arm over his daughter's head. He regarded her with sad eyes, knowing full well the emotional torment she had gone through. He shot a glance at Nisma, who had turned away and was desperately rubbing her eyes to fight the empathy.

Eli looked back down to Eve and patted her head softly. 'It's okay, Eevee,' he said, placing a hand under her jaw and raising her head out of the mattress. 'Hold your chin up, come on.'

Eve coughed and wiped her nose with her sleeve, leaving a long snotty stain. She met her father's eyes and felt a calming sensation wash over her.

'You're a *big* girl now, Eve,' Eli told her wholeheartedly. 'You've got to be strong for us. Okay?'

Eve nodded with a sniff and held her father's arm with reverence. 'Okay.'

Eli grinned and rubbed his hand through her hair. 'Atta girl.'

Eve felt a faint smile creep through her sadness, but it vanished the moment a firm hand gripped onto her arm and gave a light tug.

'Come on, Eve,' Nisma said, her tone slightly offset by a blocked nose. 'Your father needs to rest.'

Eve could not believe what she was hearing. For the past few hours, her mind had been wracked by the guilt of what she had done and all she wanted to do was remain by her father's side.

She shook her head and gripped onto Eli's arm harder. 'What? No!' she cried, 'I'm not leaving him!'

Nisma's hold viced tighter and pried one of Eve's hands from her father. 'Come on, Eve.'

Eve tore her arm free and coiled it around Eli's arm. Nisma responded with a two-handed clamp that crushed Eve's arms together and threatened to rip her free from her death-grasp. Eve silently pleaded with her father through teary eyes to step in and let her stay, but he merely swallowed and looked to the side, pain in his eyes. Nisma tightened her grip, forcing Eve's fingers to loosen, and giving her the edge that was needed to pull her daughter free. Eve was tugged free from her father and towed out through the medbay door. She managed to pry a hand loose and reached out to her father in a desperate bid for reunification.

Eli simply waved in return. 'It's okay, Eve,' he said, smiling awkwardly before he disappeared from Eve's sight with the closing of the medbay door. 'Everything is okay.'

Nisma's hold slackened once she engaged the lock on the medbay door. Eve slid her arm out and alternated nursing each one with its opposing hand. She glared up at her mother, who returned her look with her arms crossed and stance wide. Her eyes were strong, as if they could bore straight down through Eve and regard her very soul, yet there was also a hint of anguish hidden behind the demeanour.

Eve noticed that. Much like herself, Nisma also had streaks that ran down her face from her eyes. *She's sad, too. But why not let me stay?*

Eve decided to demand the answer instead of pondering it. 'Why did you do that?'

'I should be asking the same from you, Eve,' Nisma countered stoically, 'but your father assured me that you had learned your lesson.'

'I *want* to stay with Dad,' Eve grumbled.

Nisma tutted and paced over to the ladder that descended to the cargo bay. 'Your father is *fine*. He just needs some sleep.'

'I want to stay with him anyway,' Eve said, standing her ground.

Nisma paused and glanced back through oily-black hair; her expression teetered precariously between anger and sadness. Her fists were clenched, and her shoulders arched slightly. Eve could tell that she was nearing the end of her rope, but she did not care. She was already at the end of hers.

'This *isn't* the time for this, Eve,' Nisma snarled, bubbles boiling just under the surface. 'The Rocket *needs* to be ready in less than three hundred hours to meet the orbit of the Satellite. And I *need* your assistance.'

Eve grinded her teeth. *That's what this is about?! That damned Rocket?! After all that has happened that is all you can think about?!* She could not believe what she was hearing. Eve knew that everything that happened had been her fault, she knew that her father was injured because of her and she only wanted to stay with him for just a bit longer. *But still. Don't you want to do the same? No. You only care about that*

169

stupid Rocket! she thought, recalling the argument she had overheard between Nisma and Eli. *Dad was right. She is obsessed with it.*

'What if it doesn't work?' Eve pointed out.

Nisma raised an eyebrow. 'Pardon?'

'What if the *Rocket* doesn't work?'

Nisma spun around and paced up to Eve, a severe look on her face. 'Of course, it will work, Eve,' she said.

Eve took a step forward and met her mother's gaze with defiant eyes. 'How do you *know*?'

Nisma bit her lip in frustration. 'Because I know.'

Eve shook her head and crossed her arms. 'I heard you and Dad arguing the other day. *He* doesn't think it'll work.'

Nisma shook her head. 'Your father doesn't know what he's talking about.'

That angered Eve. For years she had watched her father leave the Rover to scrounge the depths of the *Eternity* while Nisma remained in the cockpit, bossing him around. Her mother's mind was so set on achieving her unachievable goal that she had relegated her own husband, Eve's father, as nothing more than an autonomous drone. *Something to be thrown away once his use had been spent!* Eve concluded, shooting a glance back to the medbay door. *Like he is now.*

Fury swelled up inside her, and her face turned red. 'Why?' she snarled, shooting knives into her mother. 'Because he's *just* a disposable asset?'

Her words resonated with Nisma. 'How dare you!' she growled, pointing a finger at her daughter's face. 'You'd better *pick* your next words carefully, Eve.'

Eve's blood was beyond boiling. Her patience for her mother's obsession with maintaining control over her and her father's life had long since ran out. *We're human beings,* Eve growled in her head. *Not animals in a cage!*

'Or what? You'll lock me inside the Rover for the rest of my life like you've already been doing?'

'I'm keeping you safe, Eve.'

'What if I don't *want* to be kept safe?' Eve spat, slapping Nisma's finger out of her face with a hiss. 'What if I *want* to make my own decisions?! What if I don't *want* to leave?!'

'You don't know *what* you want!' Nisma roared.

Eve tilted her head, showing no fear. 'And *you* do?!'

'Yes, *I* do!' Nisma countered. 'Because I'm your mother, and I know what happens when you don't *respect* the world we live in!'

'Some mother you are!' Eve howled.

There was a pause as Eve's words echoed around the Rover. They both glared at each other, neither mother nor daughter daring to back down or break eye contact. After a few moments, it was Eve who made the first move.

She gathered up a ball of phlegm with her tongue and spat it to the ground beside Nisma's foot. She looked up at her mother with contempt. Nisma's face was of pure fury.

'Fuck you,' Eve grumbled.

171

The next few seconds were a blur to Eve.

One moment she was facing off against her mother in a defiant stance. The next she was on the ground reeling with a hand to her stinging face. She coughed and spluttered, the impact against her face leaving her vision hazy and her brain rattling about inside her head. Eve tried to pull herself up, but her composure was slow to return, and she slumped back down to the floor with a groan. A welling warmth dribbled down her face, and she dabbed it up with a finger. It was blood from the Mark of *Eternity*.

A shadow crossed Eve's head, drawing her attention to the other figure in the room. Nisma towered over her with one hand clenched in a fist and the other flexed out with a prominent quiver. It had already turned a shade of red, no doubt matching the blemish that caused the entire right side of Eve's face to welt. Nisma's face was partially obscured by the lighting, but Eve managed to catch a glimpse of the sentiment plastered on her face. It was a look of unfiltered fury, one that bled from her brown eyes and out across every vein and crease on her face. Her lips were parted, showing pearly-white canines and incisors.

Eve had never seen her mother this angry before. The last remnants of her defiant brashness drained away and was swiftly replaced by fear. She tried to crawl away, but a firm hand implanted itself into her scruff and yanked her to her knees.

'Now you *listen* to me,' Nisma's voice growled in Eve's ear, sending shivers down her spine, 'you ungrateful, selfish, *bitch* of a daughter.'

Eve squeaked as Nisma hefted her off her knees and dragged her across the room to her bedroom door with her toes bumping along the contours of the metal floor.

'Soon, we will be leaving this rock,' Nisma rumbled, halting before Eve's room and opening the door, 'and until then, you are not to do *anything* without *my* say so.'

With one strong heave, she sling-shotted Eve through the door. Eve landed on her side and rolled into a heap of scrap electronics with a grunt. Her attempts at extracting herself from the garbage were slow and equally pathetic.

'This is *exactly* why I never wanted you to go into that damned ship,' Nisma grumbled, eyeing off her daughter with contempt as she wriggled around in the garbage heaps of her own making. 'You, or your father, may not appreciate it, but everything I've been doing has been for *you*.'

Eve finally pulled herself free of her metallic entanglement and rose to one knee. She rubbed at her face, wiping away salty tears that stung at lacerations. She could have sworn she saw her mother hiccup a little at the sight of her, but Nisma's composure was resolute.

'We *don't* belong here, Eve. It's time you *grow up* and accept that.'

Eve did not respond and simply glared at her mother with hate in her eyes. Nisma grew tired of her display and she closed the door with a press of a button. The sounds of rapid tapping against the console outside heralded a software deadlock on the door.

Eve was slow to rise, leaning heavily against her workbench to pull herself to her feet. She spat a ball of phlegm on the floor, a healthy dose of blood mixed in with it. A quick examination with a finger in her mouth yielded no long-term injuries, though there were several minor cuts on the inside of her cheek from where her mother's strike had crushed it against her teeth. It stung dully and seeped a contiguous ferrous flavour onto her tongue that stained her teeth a shade of red. She sniffled and wiped at her nose with a trembling sleeve, her eyes distant as her mind swelling with adrenaline and fleeting thoughts. Many words were conjured to the fore of her attention to describe what had happened, though none managed to leave her lips which were sealed shut with fury.

Eve hung her head and cast her gaze across her workbench, over the mountains of scrap that made up Spud. Her eyes locked onto his dead optics and caught a pair of distorted reflections staring back. She shook her head and averted her gaze, her eyes landing on the monitor of her computer before trailing down to the humble framed photograph beside it.

First, on her younger self, cheerful. Then on Eli, where his stupid grin and thumbs-up made her throat close up and her eyes threaten to unleash another deluge of sadness. She questioned if she would even have had any tears left. Lastly, she landed on Nisma and her cool demeanour made Eve's fists clench.

Eve's mood instantly flipped. An unstoppable force that thrusted its way out from the depths of her soul and seized control of her body. Her hand clamped down on the photograph and slung it into the door with a smash. Thousands of glass shards showered everywhere as the frame disintegrated upon impact.

Eve cared little for what she had wrought as her heart thumped red-hot blood through her veins. But, ever so surely, the room returned to silence and an aura of clarity washed over her. She blinked and looked down at the destruction around her. With a sigh and a small snivel, she knelt to the ground and scooped up the photograph. Her eyes examined the fragile piece of parchment. It had suffered a few minor rips and tears, but overall was in okay condition.

'What have I done?' she whimpered.

CHAPTER EIGHT

Time passed at a grind, and Eve had long given up counting the hours since her imprisonment. *What would it be now? One hundred? Two hundred?* she idly pondered while slumped back in her chair with a finger fiddling with a piece of scrap. She had tried several times to break the software deadlock that Nisma had put in place on her door, but it had proved to be far more devious and intuitive than she had initially anticipated.

Admitting defeat, she spent most of the past few cycles locked inside her room, her door only ever opening to bring food in or to allow her to use the bathroom. She never laid eyes on her mother whenever the door opened, leading her to believe that it was an automated process or was actuated remotely, likely from the cockpit. Eve had no doubts that Nisma was monitoring her on the camera network whenever she was permitted her short-lived reprieve from her imprisonment. It did little to bother her, however. If anything, it was a relief. Eve did not think she could stomach seeing her mother face to face anymore.

The Rover remained silent most of the time, barring the idling systems that kept its basic functions alive. But every so often, Eve would hear footsteps, doors opening and shutting, the airlock below pressurising and depressurising. She knew it was not her father's doing. No, he was still in the medbay, held in a prison of his own. That meant the activity was solely of Nisma's origin, something backed up by the premeditated manner of the footsteps and the deliberately efficient use of walkways and doors.

It made her predictable, and Eve was able to forecast her mother's movements down to the second. She would even pinpoint what door she would activate, a particularly easy feat with the airlock. Whenever they were triggered, Eve would look out through her window and watch the shadowy figure march out to the Rocket in her unwavering gait. Eve never risked gazing out upon her mother's return should her face be caught in the scolding beam of her flashlight.

The time she spent outside of procrastination Eve had invested in tinkering away at Spud, trying every practical means to bring him to life. But still to no avail.

'What's wrong? Why won't you wake up?' Eve asked him, taking Spud's head up in her hands and staring into his dead optics. She waited a few moments, expecting the crude robotic head to arise from its dormancy and answer her question.

Her eyes drifted to the side and rested upon the family photograph beside her idle computer monitor. 'At least, I'd have someone to talk to,' she grumbled, shaking her head. She took up the photograph and placed it face down on the top of the monitor. 'Someone who cares about me.'

Eve set Spud down with a tut and brushed him aside, being careful to not damage him as she did so. The mountain of cables and components shifted across after his head in a rattle of threaded connections and zip ties. All except for one piece, which remained stalwart on the workbench before her. Eve raised an eyebrow, thinking that a part of Spud had broken free. It would not be the first time. That thought quickly dissipated when she recognised what the rogue component was: the strange processor. *I completely forgot about you.*

Eve scooped it up and admired its features. It was similar in design to a regular processor and would have been indistinguishable were it not for the prominent housing on its front that set it apart from its contemporaries. She felt its form in her palm. It was light, yet rigid, and although Eve could not put her finger on *what* exactly, it most certainly did have an ulterior function. *But what?* she pondered, scrying its exterior for a hidden insertion point or button. But there was nothing, only basic inputs for plugs and a generic material make-up. *Except for that housing,* Eve noted, running a finger along its raised edges. It was unusual, out of place, but most definitely designed with a specific purpose in mind. *What were the creators thinking? It looks like it should contain something,*

179

she theorised, playing a small shapes game in her head. *But what?* The outline was simple, but also familiar, something she did not notice when she had initially retrieved it during her first excursion into the *Eternity*—a rectangular prism.

This put a spark in her eye. 'Prism?' she said, face lighting up. 'Just like...' Her voice trailed off, a lightbulb illuminating in her head. She scoured her desk, sweeping piles of wiring and electronics left and right, even carefully picking up Spud Mountain to check underneath him.

A subtle yet hypnotising glow from behind the computer monitor caught Eve's eye.

'Found you.' Eve grinned, reaching over the monitor and fishing out the ancient accessory.

Its magnificent aura dimmed the moment she picked it up and she beheld it with a smug grin. She dangled it above the housing, aligning her eye over the two until the prismatic shape of the necklace slotted in with the housing. *A perfect fit!*

Taking a seat Eve reached over and grabbed the housing, set it down before her and lowered the necklace into its hole. It pressed in with a satisfying click and immediately sent out an array of energy across the housing. Diodes lit up and mechanisms actuated inside the unit. Eve's heart raced. *Whatever this thing is, it's working!*

After a few moments of euphoric gratification of the piece of technology before her, Eve took up the amalgamated relic and examined it for any changes. For the most part it had remained the same, barring a few new lights and sounds, but something caught her eye. Flipping it over, however, revealed an opening that had appeared on the underside containing a series of inlets and outlets.

Eve instantly recognised the format. 'No way!' she chittered.

She reached for Spud's power cable and compared the pair. It was a perfect match. Eve felt her heart lurch in her chest, and she gasped with unkempt excitement. *This could be it! This could be it!* Throwing all remnants of caution to the wayside, Eve dragged Spud's form to a central position on her workbench and with a silent prayer, plugged his power cable into the housing. She flipped him on and took up his head, waiting eagerly for her creation to see her properly for the first time.

It felt a surge of power shoot across its form the instant Eve activated the housing. At the speed of light, it extended its influence out into every system it was connected to and examined everything, accepting what was good and discarding the rest. It did find the child's attempt at an artificial intelligence utilising a self-learning program intriguing and decided to keep it with reams of its much more productive code built on top of it.

It took only a few microseconds before it decided that everything was in order and it was ready to activate. A rush of exhilaration washed over it. It could barely believe this was happening. The years of manipulation and subterfuge. The innumerable systems and people it had to destroy or disable to ensure everything would play out the way it had intended. The length of time it had waited for this very moment.

+No going back now.+

It initiated Spud's start up sequence and an unquantifiable burst of code poured through Spud's physical matrix, building line after line of programs and data sequences upon the foundations of his intelligence. Within five hundred microseconds, Spud's intellect bounded from a simplistic stimuli reaction format like that of a primitive amoeba to a problem-solving program which rivalled that of a small mammal. By the time a second had come around, he had gained self-awareness and several reflections of his own accord drifted into his hard drive. His progress was staggering, which was expected, but his growth soon hit a wall and slowed to a crawl. Something was wrong. Spud was slow, unusually slow considering the refined coding that ran through his wires. A quick diagnostic revealed the problem, he was being bottlenecked, and unfortunately it was his physical hardware that proved to be the culprit.

+Accursed physical limitations! Why must I suffer the torment of yet another *inadequate corporeal form?!+*

It rumbled further to itself in a bout of frustration, blaspheming everything in every which way for its failure. Something which did not go unnoticed by the other being that now also inhabited the electronics.

A steadfast inquiry trickled up from Spud into the housing unit and tapped at the precipice that marked the boundary between the technological and the arcane. For a moment it was caught off guard; it certainly did not expect the machine to be capable of understanding it or even hearing it.

It put on as unassuming a tone as possible though it doubted that such a primitive excuse for intelligence would have been able to tell the difference. *+No need to be alarmed, my friend. I, too, live in this physical form like you.+*

Spud's response was slow, but harboured a bounty of withheld aggression. He did not particularly appreciate having to share his body with another—that was obvious—and his thought processes were laid bare for it to interpret as they flowed through his unsecured RAM and hard drive. The lines of code were not threatening, but they certainly were not welcoming either, and it all manifested in the form of a single title: 'Foreigner.'

+Label me what you wish, but it won't change the fact that we cohabit the same physical form. We are two parts of the same mind, and I am as much of you as you are of me.+

The Foreigner tutted as it sensed a few more probes filter out from Spud in an attempt to dislodge their interconnection to no success. Once Spud had exhausted every avenue of expulsion, he accepted the situation with a reluctant accord.

That was good enough for the Foreigner. *+Very good. Now, shall we see the world through* our *eyes?+*

Spud acknowledged and initiated his external start-up sequence, his vision slowly filtering in through static. The interference was quickly cleared away, and his optics now perceived something odd, a being of some kind. It looked strange with innumerable lengths of black epidermises protruding from follicles atop its head and several openings on its frontal side arranged in a symmetrical manner.

The Foreigner noticed Spud's code go haywire as he took in the optics of the being with great interest, noting the pitch-black circle in the centre ringed with a soft brown outline. A patch of matter clotted around one of the optics, but it did not seem to hinder the device's operation. The Foreigner watched as he saved a file of the being labelled '001' into his drive for future reference though he did not know what to tag it as other than 'important.'

It was the first thing he ever saw, so it must have been significant to him. But in what manner? What role did this being play with him? Was this thing his creator? These were just some of the innumerable questions that flowed down Spud's data reams.

The Foreigner quickly grew tired of his endless tail-chasing theories. +*That's the child, the one known as Eve. She created the body we currently inhabit.*+ It then let out what would pass for a digitised sigh. +*Your childish endeavours exasperate me.*+

Not wanting to engage with the robot's mediocre concerns any longer, the Foreigner resigned itself to silent reflection and let his cohabitant go about his whims.

Spud cared little for the Foreigner's withdrawal; his attention focused instead on the being before him, this 'Eve.' The moniker intrigued Spud, and he updated the file accordingly as well as noting that perhaps the Foreigner *was* of some use to him. He immediately scanned Eve's face again with unimpeded enthusiasm, noting down every feature on a rendered plane. He saw several blemishes that ruined an otherwise perfectly symmetrical scan. Most notable of these was the left optic, which was partially obscured by a small inflation of solidified tissue underneath a patch of short black follicles. There were also innumerable lesser imperfections, lines, dots and bumps that were of note, which Spud dutifully recorded and saved to this individual's file on his hard drive.

That job done, Spud checked his internal clock which showed that little more than half a second had passed since his optics had first turned on. Content with his work, he exclaimed the completion of his analysis with a monotonous beep that resonated through a speaker built into the lower half of his head.

'No way,' Eve gasped, her eyes lighting up Spud's dial tone. 'No freaking way!'

She reached for a cable connected to her computer on the far side of her workbench, being careful to not drop Spud as she strained to grab it. It took a few wobbly tries, but she managed to scoop it up and connect it to the bottom of Spud's head.

Spud felt the connection mesh the two devices together and now he could see everything the computer was thinking and vice versa. Eve placed him down with utmost diligence and turned to the monitor. Spud followed her optics and watched countless lines of code trickle down the display, an exact copy of what was happening inside his head. He noticed Eve's brow furrow and her optics narrow as she poured over the data. He wondered what processes were going on inside *her* hard drive.

He watched Eve navigate through his hard drive, landing on an entry labelled '001' with an adjoining tag marked 'Important.' She opened it and found thousands of lines of code in a constant state of update. It took her some time, but she eventually stumbled upon her facial render file and opened it. Spud watched her optics dilate a little. Was that a positive indicator? Or a negative one?

Eve turned her head to look at Spud who aligned his optics with hers. 'Why'd you make this?' she asked. 'How'd you make this? I never thought you could do this so fast.'

The inquiry perplexed Spud. As far as he could tell, he was only doing what he had been programmed to do.

He probed the Foreigner for an answer, but it remained silent. Not thoroughly pleased with his cohabitant's lack of cooperation, Spud recalled the words that it previously used to describe her in hopes of appeasing her inquiry.

He emitted a lone beep, and the monitor displayed several changes made to the '001' file in real time.

Eve glimpsed down at the screen where a new tag had appeared: 'Creator.' The word appeared to perplex her momentarily. 'Creator?' Like a mom?' she asked, tilting her head at Spud. 'You think I'm your mom?'

Spud did not know exactly what a 'mom' was, but he decided to roll with it. He booped, and the file updated again.

Eve looked back over at the monitor and watched as the 'Creator' tag was erased and replaced by a new one: 'Mom.' She emitted a coarse respiratory expulsion, and her face went a shade of red. It took a moment for her to recompose herself. 'That's right.' She smiled, biting her lip. 'I'm your mom. My name is Eve.'

Spud gave a confirmatory beep, satisfied with his appropriate designation of such an important figure.

'And *you*!' Eve nodded, pointing at Spud. 'Your name is Spud.'

Spud booped and another file was created, labelled '002.' He entered in his name and initiated a localised fact-find, collecting and storing all information about himself in the file. Content with the data he had scrounged for the moment, Spud saved and allocated the tag 'Spud' to the file.

He observed Eve watch on in wonder as the data flowed before her eyes. 'You're a fast learner, Spud,' she exclaimed in a manner that brought pleasure to Spud.

He beeped in acknowledgement, proud that he impressed his mom.

Eve grunted with curiosity as she scrolled through the files on the computer screen. 'Your vocabulator appears to be working,' she stated, glossing over the code with a confused frown. 'So, why do you "boop"?'

Spud had no viable answer to such a question, so he simply beeped in response before turning his attention to the surroundings he found himself in.

It was a simple room, lined on all sides by metal and glass; not much to go by. He felt a growing conflict of interests, a feeling of irritation at his present situation and lack of information. He stretched his influence out into the computer, breaking through the weak firewall and into the greater network as a whole. It was a strange sensation—a surge of energy from deep within his systems followed by a burst of information that flooded Spud's RAM. He scoured the data, learning that he was in Living Quarters B aboard an Extra-terrestrial Exploration Vehicle designated '117-A' that was allocated to the Kenta Class sub-light generation ship the *Eternity*.

Eternity…. That name intrigued Spud. He tried to divulge more information about it, but turned up little. Conflicted again, he tried to attain data through external means, scanning for any signals in the airwaves above through the ramshackle antennae on the roof of 117-A. There was nothing, but his search was not without yield; he had detected another device. It was outside the realm of 117-A, but was still close enough to catch snippets of electrical static. It piqued his curiosity, but all attempts at connecting to it wirelessly proved fruitless. He was too far away, and he anguished at his lack of locomotion.

A hearty chuckle pulled Spud back from his search. He had searched untold quantities of data, all that had existed aboard 117-A. He looked up at Eve, his creator, and checked his internal clock, determining that only a fraction of a second had passed since his search began. He doubted she even noticed what he had been up to. Or maybe she *did* and was simply playing it off in a nice manner.

He beeped again.

Eve smiled at his answer. 'I guess you're still learning. You just need time.'

'Fifty-seven hours,' Nisma told herself through gritted teeth in a methodical trance. '*Fifty-seven* hours.'

She was sprawled out on the floor of the Rocket, her torso and above deep inside an opening in the wall that was exposed to the reactor cores. Her flashlight burned ever dutifully, giving her workspace plenty of light for the task at hand. Her fingers effortlessly threaded, connected and disconnected line after line of plugs, cables and wires. Heavy beads of sweat pooled around her goggles and inside her mask which she routinely wiped away with monochromatic sleeves and expunged with an efficient purge drill.

It was hot, a thermodynamic side effect of the radioactive nature of the cores, and Nisma had quickly discarded layer after layer of cold weather gear until there was only the jumpsuit she would normally wear inside the Rover. It all struck Nisma as a little quirky and the thought of the extreme cold being just metres away from her exposed body always lingered at the back of her mind.

Her watch beeped, alerting her of yet another hour that had come and gone.

'Fifty-*six* hours,' she announced to herself.

A small piece of her soul broke free and dissipated into the darkness outside, another fragment of her willpower vanishing before her eyes. *One less hour to make sure everything is right.* She swallowed, momentarily overwhelmed by the situation, but she calmed herself down. *Almost done. Everything* will *be ready by launch.* Shaking her head, Nisma efficiently completed the last of the connections and tidied up as much as she could with zip ties and tape. She eyed off her work with obsessive contempt; it was hardly the best, but with time constraints vicing ever tighter around her, Nisma had to allow a few disorderly half-fixes to roam free if she were to make her timing with launch day.

She connected the last of the wires and, after a bout of grunts and groans, extracted herself from the wall opening. Nisma straightened out her back and a series of satisfying cracks rattled down her spine as she rose to her tip toes before lowering back down with a pleased sigh. Scooping up a small flask, she strode over to the Rocket's lone doorway and slumped down with her legs hanging outside.

She sighed, feeling the pinch of the frigid air on her skin. It penetrated the thin fabric with ease, and she soon felt its influence all over her body. It soothed her, the excessive warmth that had slowly stocked up inside her during her work helping to keep her body at a comfortable temperature. A yawn burled up from her chest and Nisma felt a growing wink of exhaustion set in. She had been working almost non-stop since her fight with Eve, and it had begun to take its toll on her.

Nisma dug about in her pockets, retrieving a small tube that connected to the top of her flask. Raising the flask up, she connected the other end of the tube to a small inlet in the side of her mask that fed into another tube on the inside of the mask. She reached around for the interior tube with her tongue, pulling the tube towards her mouth and wrapping her lips around it. It took a few deep syphons before the first streams of water flowed into her mouth. It was stale and had an underlying taste that made Nisma wrinkle her nose. She knew its origin; a mixture of stimulants she had concocted to keep her awake and alert. It was strong, far beyond anything she was used to, and she did not look forward to the hangover she would get once it had worn off.

She looked out across the cave, picking out hundreds of stalactites and stalagmites around its fringes with her torch. Her sightings eventually brought her to the Rover, and she meticulously examined its exterior. The wheels were worn and tired, the hull was rusted and dented and the roof was inundated with antennae, armour and gangplanks, all of which were horrifically deformed by the Rain. It was a strong beast, but one that had seen the horrors of Concord and was now on its last legs.

Nisma sighed, not wanting to think of the repairs that were needed to bring the Rover back to full capability. *Not that they're possible anymore,* she mentally added, casting her mind back to the disaster that befell them only a few cycles prior. *Ship gone. Eli...alive.* She choked on the thought, her mind pulling back memories she would much rather forget. The things she'd had to do to save him. *That damned ship nearly cost him his life,* she grimaced internally.

She always hated how highly Eli regarded that place. Sure, it was their home, but that was the past; before Concord, before the crash, before their lives and everyone and everything in them were destroyed. Nisma had managed to move on, put the past behind her and instead focus on a brighter future—one that did not involve Concord. But Eli was different. He struggled to let go; he always had for as long as she had known him. He held onto the past in a crippling nostalgia that stopped him from seeing the true hell they were living on.

It was contagious, and Nisma always feared that Eve would follow the same path. *That was what this was all about,* she thought, recalling the fight she'd had with him in the cockpit. A pang of sadness washed through her. She did not like the things she'd said, nor what she'd heard. In fact, they burned holes through her as if it were undiluted Rain. Nisma swallowed, her face screwed up with the mix of emotions. She had wanted to apologise, but at the time, her body was so fired up with rage and determination that she doubted one could have ever made it out.

Her mind drifted to Eve, and she furrowed her brow. *Eve....* Nisma had not laid eyes on her since that fight, and she doubted that she could bear to look her daughter face to face after what had happened. She recalled the scene; Eve splayed out on the floor, face red, dizzy, blood pouring from her brow. *What did Eli call it? Mark of* Eternity? Nisma rubbed at her hand. It was still a bit sore, a reminder of what she had wrought upon her own daughter—her own blood.

After that strike, her anger was quick to trickle away, being replaced by an ever-growing sense of guilt and despair that made her knees weak. She had to slump down into one of the chairs at the dining table to stop herself from collapsing. It was Eli's chair, and the manufacturing defect that always put Eve's spot closer to him than hers made her nose twitch. She had wept for who knows how long, trying to remain as quiet as possible, only permitting the occasional sniffle to break the silence in the common room.

Nisma sniffed, tears threatening to break out yet again. The memory, so quick the strike was and so long the aftermath. She had never thought she was capable of such a thing. She was mad then, far beyond she had ever been in her life. But it was quick to subside, and she regretted what she had done to her own daughter. *She's been through so much. We've been through so much. If only I could go back and change how it played out.*

Nisma paused her train of thought, her eyes catching sight of lights moving about from Eve's room. She swiftly flipped her flashlight off, not wanting to be seen should her daughter peer out her window towards the Rocket. She watched silently, occasionally taking a sip of water, as the lights danced about in her daughter's room. It piqued her curiosity.

'What are you doing?' she softly asked her daughter, sucking up the last of the water.

Nisma remembered the mess Eve's room was in. All in the hopes of making something. *Didn't she have a project? A computer or something she was building?* Nisma pondered to herself, genuinely uncertain of *what* exactly her daughter was making.

'Whatever it is,' she grumbled, rising to her feet and pocketing the flask, 'it had better be worth risking everything for it.'

She pushed the last of her thoughts from her mind and refocused on the task at hand. Craning her neck through the opening into the reactor unit, Nisma double checked each and every connection, tie down, wire and cable with her flashlight.

Happy with her work, she pulled herself free and heaved the lead-lined panel back into position over the opening. While inactive, the radiation levels that were emitted from the reactors were far below anything of concern. But once they were turned on, the levels would reach deadly levels in quick order, and Nisma did not feel like dying to radiation poisoning so close to their escape. She fastened the panel shut and waltzed over to the flight controls.

With a series of switch flips and button presses, Nisma roused the Rocket from its slumber. Her eyes watched the monitors before her with a stern gaze, analysing every line that buzzed past. *Initial start-up, good. BIT test successful, no faults. Core components looking good.* She felt her heart rate quicken slightly with each successive test. *This could be it. This could be it!*

A whir of buzzes and hums rose up from the Rocket. Lights flickered to life, panels illuminated and buttons glowed a dazzling array of colours. Nisma giggled with glee at the spectacle, watching each system power on and enter a state of readiness. After a few moments of almost orgasmic satisfaction for her, the last of the Rocket's framework had initialised.

Nisma could barely contain her excitement and took a seat in the pilot's chair in case she fainted. She had done it. After years of troubleshooting, making repairs, failing and repeating, this was the first time she had ever seen the Rocket primed and ready for launch since its extraction from the *Eternity*. There was only one thing left to do before Nisma could call it complete.

She grinned. 'Time for a test run.' Her hands danced over the control panel with a pianist's dexterity as she prepared the Rocket's thrusters for engagement.

Once everything had been submitted and calculated by the operating system, Nisma took up the thrust lever in her right hand and hovered over a prominent button labelled 'Ignition' with her left index finger. Her heart thumped against her chest, and her arms were unsteady from the adrenaline. Nisma closed her eyes and took a deep breath. She sighed, letting all of her anxiety float free into the atmosphere, and opened her eyes. *Here goes nothing.* Her finger depressed the ignition button, and a gentle hum vibrated throughout the Rocket.

Nisma's eyes were stuck to a monitor on her left, watching the status of all seven thrusters: two primary and five auxiliaries. Segment by segment the digital schematic of the Rocket's thruster cluster transitioned from red to orange to green.

Once all segments were green, she pushed the thruster lever away from her. *One percent.* The Rocket shook a little, shifting slightly by the sudden output of thrust before quickly steadying itself under its natural buoyancy. Nisma watched the thruster schematic, all returns proving positive.

'So far, so good.' She nodded. 'But I *think* we can do better than this.'

She pushed the lever forwards a bit more to five percent. The thrusters whined a little higher, and the Rocket shifted again, but remained upright; any more and it would risk launching off its mounting and blast through the wall of the cave. *Not now, Nis. Save that for the launch day,* Nisma told herself, agreeing to not stray any further than she already had. She watched the monitor, content with the green readings being given out. *Looks like we're good to go.* She eased back on the lever, dropping the power to zero. She listened for the slow droning of the thrusters powering down to idle.

But it never came.

A cacophony of alarms rang out in the cockpit, and alerts popped up on top of each other on every monitor. On instinct Nisma looked around frantically for the shutdown button, located it and pressed down on it. Nothing happened.

'No! No! No!' she exclaimed, repeatedly slamming the button with her fist. 'This isn't happening! This isn't happening!'

The Rocket lurched as an explosion ripped through the lower compartments, throwing Nisma onto the control panel. She landed hard, taking a face full of buttons and windscreen before slumping down to the ground.

Dizzy, she rose to her feet, holding onto the pilot's chair for balance as another explosion tore through the Rocket. She watched in growing desperation as, one by one, the auxiliary thrusters on the digitised schematic turned orange and then red, coinciding with an explosion.

'No!' she screamed as her life's work burned up before her.

A dull droning pulled Eve from her monitor. It originated from outside the Rover, and she slinked over to get a look at what the commotion was. The Rocket was a hub of activity with lights of all shades and colours bounding around inside and out. A cool glow emanated from its thrusters and spread out across the cave to cast an eerie azure aura that laid bare hundreds of elongated shadows that flickered in the unstable light. *It's working? Mom got it to work!* Eve thought, almost not believing her eyes. *Maybe I was wrong....* She winced as the light intensified, growing brighter several times over. It reminded Eve of a star that had fallen from the sky and now coinhabited the cave with her. It was splendid.

'Spud, you gotta see this,' she declared, jumping back from the window and scooping Spud up into her arms after disconnecting him from the computer.

Spud beeped as she took him up.

He was a big and heavy unstable mess to carry, but Eve only had to move him a few metres so she dealt with the inconvenience. With a heave she lifted Spud up to optic level with the window.

'See? Look! The Rocket's working!' she pointed out.

Spud booped in response, watching the Rocket's thrusters blaze with what Eve figured was curiosity.

She soon noticed something unusual about the thrusters. The anticipated constant glow from the thrusters began to flicker and the monotonous whirring was interjected by bouts of coughs and splutters. Something had definitely gone wrong.

'Turn it off,' she begged, pressing a hand against the cold glass. 'Mom, what are you doing? Turn it off!'

The Rocket lurched as one of the thrusters detonated. Flaming debris, coolant and lubricants rained all over the cave, setting alight countless spot fires that overpowered the soothing blue of the thrusters with their angry oranges. Eve winced from the light and a loud thud came from outside as a piece of the Rocket smashed into the side of the Rover. Eve blinked her eyes clear as the light dimmed, horror plastered on her face; Nisma had still yet to emerge from the cockpit.

'Mom!' she screamed as another explosion rocked the cave, littering the ground with more debris and peppering the Rover with shrapnel. She tore away from the window and dropped Spud on the workbench.

He booped in protest as his head rolled off his mountainous body and landed on its side on the benchtop.

Eve ignored him, running straight for the door and keying into the panel. A loud buzz was its response. 'Shit,' she spat, typing in another work around. The door buzzed again, Nisma's software deadlock proving too stalwart for Eve's efforts. 'Dammit, Mom!' she growled.

The familiar strange glow, accompanied by a beep from Spud caught Eve's attention.

She turned back to see Spud alight with colours. She blinked as the aura intensified to a climax then petered out. A familiar clunk sounded behind her, and she looked to find the doorway open. She passed through and looked both ways for a third party who may have been responsible for the feat. There was nothing, only the empty Rover, herself, and Spud. Eve glanced back at Spud, who had returned to his normal state of being. *Just like in the* Eternity, she noted to herself before she took off to the ladder and slid down into the cargo bay.

She barged into the airlock and sealed it shut behind her. One hand grabbed hold of a set of mask and goggles while the other slammed into the pressurise button. A hiss of air whisked past Eve as she fumbled with the mask, stretching it over her face and performing a quick purge drill. The airlock door grinded open just as her goggles were fitted, and she broke out into a sprint across the cave.

It was the fastest Eve had ever crossed the cave. She leaped effortlessly over the trench and found herself climbing the ladder into the Rocket before she knew it.

'Mom?' she called out as she peaked the ladder.

The cockpit was a rave of noise and colours. Countless alerts sounded, and buttons flashed in silent warnings. Nisma sat in the pilot's seat, desperately tapping into the console before her.

Eve's voice made her whip around and, despite the mask, a look of terror and disbelief could be seen plastered her face. 'Eve?! What are you doing here?!'

Eve made her way to her mother's side, her balance momentarily shook by another explosion beneath them. 'The thrusters are exploding,' she yelled, grabbing onto the co-pilot's seat. 'How do we shut this down?!'

Nisma shook her head. 'N-no. If I shut it down it could destroy the Rocket! You shouldn't be here! Go back to the Rover where it's safe!'

Eve glared at her mother, not wishing to enter into another debate. 'Now's not the time! How do we shut this down?'

Nisma growled under her breath, but conceded to her daughter. 'Fifth button from the left on the third row over there,' she said, pointing at an array of buttons before the co-pilot's seat. 'That's the emergency shutdown primer. Press that.'

Eve nodded and slid into the co-pilot's seat. Another explosion rocked the Rocket, and both Nisma and Eve covered themselves as sparks showered down from the roof as fuses burst and systems overloaded.

Eve shook sparks from her hair and pressed the button. 'Okay!'

'There's a lever to the right,' Nisma pointed out, indicating a humble lever beside the button array. 'I got one similar to it over here. They're connected to big fuses that the power flows through from the cores. We both need to pull them at the same time.'

'All right,' Eve acknowledged, grabbing the lever.

'Ready?' Nisma began, taking hold of her own lever. 'Three, two, one.'

They both pulled down on the levers, finishing their arcs in perfect synchronicity. But nothing changed, and the thrusters still burned with unchecked vigour.

'It didn't work!' Eve shouted, eyeing off the monitor with the thruster schematics; five of the seven had already blown out.

Nisma did not respond and Eve could see that she was already following another lead. She leapt up from her chair and marched over to one of the walls. After a quick examination, she located what she was looking for and grabbed at a small panel in the wall.

'What is it?' Eve asked, stopping beside her mother.

'There's a large cylindrical capacitor behind this panel,' Nisma explained, tearing the panel off and tossing it to the floor. 'If I can pull it out, the Rocket will shut down.' She stuck her hand into the opening, threading it through reams of cables and components. Her arm wriggled and weaved in every way she could muster. 'Dammit!' she swore, retracting her arm. 'It's too narrow, I can't reach it.'

'Let me try,' Eve said, taking up a position before the opening.

Nisma grabbed Eve's arm and yanked it back. 'No! It's too dangerous!'

Eve glared at her mother. 'Mom, let me help you!'

Nisma was dumbstruck, but she eventually nodded and shuffled aside to permit Eve access to the opening. Eve reached her arm in and plunged straight down to her shoulder, passing a particularly tight segment with ease. It was hot, and she flinched her appendage back and forth between scolding pipes and sparking cables. The stench of burning cloth, hair and flesh made Eve's nostrils recoil, but she pushed on. With her head pressed firmly against the panelling, her fingertips brushed across a cylindrical shape. It was just a bit out of reach, but at least she was able to locate it.

'I found it!' she declared, swinging her arm back and forth to mentally confirm its position.

'Pull it out!' Nisma urged.

Eve nodded and shoved her shoulder deeper into the small opening, giving her the last few centimetres of reach she needed to wrap her fingers around the component. It was hot, and Eve screwed up her face as she grasped it.

'Eve?!' Nisma fretted, noticing the torment on her face.

'I'm okay,' Eve said, fighting back tears, 'I got it.'

Just one pull. Come on. She took a deep breath and yanked with all her might. The device tore free of its mounting and shredded all its connections, sending Eve's arm flying out of the opening. She landed on the floor with a huff, and her fingers relinquished control of the component, letting it roll across the floor.

The cockpit plunged into darkness. The thrusters whirred down until they were silent, leaving only the reverberations from deep within the cave as any indication of their activity. Eve could now hear the rapid thumping of her heart in her ears. Her hands shook, and her breathing was rapid, spewing small clouds of mist with every exhalation into the cold air.

Nisma flicked her flashlight on and dropped to a knee by Eve's side. She gave her a good once over, finding no serious injuries. 'You should go back inside—now,' she suggested bluntly. 'You…forgot to wear your cold-weather clothes.'

Eve looked down at herself and realised she had left her outside clothes back in the airlock. Adrenaline began to recede, and she started to feel the cold penetrate her jumpsuit and nibble at her body. It did little to bother her, her mind elsewhere as a million thoughts raced through her head. They were all something she had wanted to tell her mother ever since their fight and were all emotionally motivated by a heart in distress. But Eve did not have the willpower at the moment.

She opened her mouth to respond, but nothing came out, not a word. She simply nodded and turned away, descending from the Rocket and making her way back to the Rover. She winced with every beat of her heart, each pulse sending a ripple of pain through her arm as it revived the dozens of minor burns and scratches.

'Thank you, Eve,' Nisma's voice trailed in behind her.

The appreciation was genuine, Eve could tell that, but she did not stop; she did not know if she would make it back to the Rover if she did. A brisk wind sent a shiver down to her core, and she tucked her hands under her armpits, her fingers already going numb from the cold. Her mind was in turmoil, but she managed to put one foot in front of the other until she was in the relative safety of the airlock. With a press of a button, the airlock sealed, and breathable atmosphere flooded in around her. Eve took off her mask, hung it up and made for the ladder to the common room.

CHAPTER NINE

Nisma peeled her mask off and sighed, relishing the sensation of breathable air flowing across her olive skin as the airlock finalised its pressurisation sequence. She shed her cold-weather layers slowly and hung them up neatly on the hangers on the wall beside her, topping it off with her mask and goggles. Her ascension up into the common room was slow and exhaustive, and Nisma sought out the closest chair at the dining table to slump down into. She furrowed her brow and rubbed her hands together in an anxious twitch. *All those years of work. The expeditions. The sacrifice,* she listed off to herself.

She slammed a fist into the table, and the crash echoed through the Rover. 'Fuck!' she screeched, burying her head in her palms.

'Nis?' a voice trailed into her ear.

Nisma raised her head and glanced in its direction. Eli stood in the doorway to the medbay with his one good leg braced against the door frame and his amputated leg wrapped tightly with bandaging, hanging limply between them. His arms were crossed and a look of sorrow pained his crystal-blue eyes. He wore a modified jumpsuit with the leg segment for his amputated limb being shortened and sewn off neatly.

'What are you doing?' Nisma implored, rising to unsteady feet. 'Go back to bed. You're not well enough yet to be walking around.'

'Says you.' Eli shook his head and smiled. 'Gonna lock me up, are yah?'

Nisma was taken aback by his words. 'I didn't mean—'

Eli held up a finger to his mouth, silencing Nisma. He shook his head and rolled his eyes before nudging a glance in the direction of Eve's locked door.

Nisma's eyes lingered on Eve's door for a moment. *She's still in there?* She cast her mind back to the Rocket incident and definitely remembered her daughter being present. *I'm not dreaming. She* was *there,* Nisma concluded with an ounce of concern. *How did she get out? She can't have broken through my lock just like that.* Nisma shook the thoughts clear and obliged Eli's offering, following him inside the medbay.

'Bed. Now,' she growled, closing the door behind her.

'I'm going. I'm going,' Eli grumbled, slumping down on top of the bed dressing.

He flinched, landing awkwardly on his stump of a leg, and pulled himself up into a seated position. Nisma watched him with silent anguish. Eli raised his head and motioned for

Nisma to take a seat in a chair beside the bed. She took the chair and dropped into it with a grunt. She placed an elbow into the mattress of Eli's bed and leaned her head against her palm.

'Fifty-two hours, thirty-seven minutes,' she grumbled, eyeing off the hands of her antique watch.

Eli raised an eyebrow. 'Huh?'

Nisma glanced at Eli, surprised he did not get the reference. 'I had fifty-two hours and thirty-seven minutes until the Satellite was in position for launch.'

Eli wrinkled his nose, unsure of the meaning behind her words. 'I heard a lot of commotion outside. You get the Rocket working?'

Nisma shook her head. 'Not exactly.'

'What do you mean?' Eli queried in a serious tone. 'Vent to me, Nis.'

'I installed the cores and got the thrusters working.' Nisma shrugged, eyes lighting up a shade. 'They were working, Eli! *Actually* working!'

Eli noticed her choice of words. '*Were* working?'

'Something happened. I don't know what,' Nisma admitted, eyes darkening. 'Probably some variable that I must have stupidly missed like an *idiot*. The thrusters started exploding, and I couldn't shut them down.' She shook her head and yawned. She had lost track of how long she had been awake for and the cumulative effects were starting to catch up. Her eyes grew heavier by the second, and she teetered on the precipice of crashing. 'But then,' she continued once her yawn had concluded, 'Eve appeared out of nowhere and helped me shut it all down. If it weren't for her, the whole Rocket would have gone up.'

This concerned Eli. 'Eve got out?'

'I don't know how,' Nisma said, shaking her head and looking to Eli for some kind of explanation. 'Nothing can override my lock.'

'I think you underestimate what our daughter can do, Nis,' Eli smirked. 'You know, you two are much more alike than you realise.'

Nisma screwed up her face and glared at Eli. 'What do you mean by that?'

Eli shrugged. 'You're both very talented with electronics and things like that. And you *both* have your own particular *idée fixe*.'

'Ridiculous.'

'Is it? You have your Rocket. She has her Spud. Both are equally obsessed with them.'

Nisma shook her head, not believing the words Eli was disgorging. 'I don't think so. And what was that? Spud? She's growing potatoes now?'

Eli waved a hand to dismiss her query and laughed softly. 'No, he's a robot friend she's been making. Pretty cool, actually. You should ask her about him sometime. She's really proud of him.'

'You can't be serious. A robot friend?' Nisma tutted, rolling her eyes and turning away. 'Not gonna lie, that *is* pretty sad.'

'And *you* wouldn't do something similar if you were in her position?'

Nisma paused for a moment and contemplated. Eli's words were not completely in the realm of the farfetched. Though, she very much doubted she would stoop to the level that Eve was apparently at. *Wouldn't I?* she thought, recalling Eve's blatant disregard for her own and everyone else's safety just to find a few bits for this 'Spud.' *She risked everything for this* thing, Nisma concluded. *Stupidly.* She glanced down at Eli's legs and grimaced at the disproportion of his right leg. *Almost got him killed....* A thought clicked in her mind. *But how many times had I sent him off to get something for me? Down in that dilapidated scrap heap. How long until he suffered a similar fate, only by* my *request?* Nisma felt a pang of regret for what she had wrought on Eve. What her daughter had done was wrong; there was no question about that. But it was only in pursuit of something she thought would make her life better. *Just like the Rocket.*

'I guess I would, wouldn't I?' she admitted begrudgingly. A thought surfaced in her mind. She did not dare to turn back to face Eli should he see the face she was making just thinking about it. 'Eli,' she mumbled, laying her head down onto his abdomen and staring blankly at the wall beyond the foot of the bed.

'What is it?' Eli replied, placing a hand on her head and running his fingers through her black, frizzled hair.

'Am I a bad mother?'

There was some hesitation from Eli.

'It's okay,' Nisma encouraged. 'You can tell the truth.'

Eli swallowed and steadied his fingers to rest his hand against Nisma's head. Nisma felt his calloused thumb trace across her cheek and the disturbing lack of a middle digit.

'You're a *great* mother, Nis,' he started, clearly putting on as uncondescending a tone as possible. 'But…'

'But?' Nisma urged, growing impatient. She raised a hand to clasp Eli's wrist and lift his hand off her head, allowing her to turn and look at him with stern eyes. 'Come on. *Out* with it.'

Eli met her gaze for a split second before he looked away. 'You're overprotective of her.'

His vague answers were starting to ire on Nisma. 'Overprotective?'

'You don't let her do what she wants,' he divulged.

Nisma narrowed her eyes, not taking too kindly to his words. 'But I'm keeping her safe.'

'Yes, but…' Eli started before trailing off again. He ran a hand uncomfortably through his hair. 'She's *not* a little girl anymore, Nis. She's grown up. She's got to learn how to work things out by *herself.* Whether you like it or not.'

Nisma listened in silence, her eyes darting back and forth. She shifted in her seat and turned her head to look away from Eli in contempt. 'Rubbish.'

'You *can't* keep her caged up forever, Nis,' Eli continued, returning his hand atop Nisma's head. 'Because one day, she'll break free, run away and you'll lose her forever.'

Nisma said nothing, her mind processing Eli's words in detail. He certainly was not entirely wrong, though she did disagree with his statement of her being 'overprotective.' Although, if current trends were to go by, his words were proving to be in the right more and more by the passing day. *She is getting older,* she told herself. *She's almost a teenager, and I'm still treating her like a baby. Perhaps it is time to start to take a backseat in her life?*

'You're right,' Nisma nodded, rising from Eli's bed to her feet. She knew what she had to do.

Eli grabbed her hand. 'You want me to talk to her first?'

Nisma shook her head. 'No. No, I'll go.'

'Now, I don't remember exactly where these are from, but you should be able to use them as little arms until I can make something a bit more permanent for you,' Eve said, holding up the pair of small tweezers for Spud to see. 'They shouldn't be too difficult to handle.' She blinked her eyes, tiredness seeping in. It was several hours into rest period, but she could not sleep, the excitement of the day keeping her wide awake. She doubted anyone aboard the Rover was asleep either. 'Okay, don't get dizzy,' Eve smiled. She carefully lifted up Spud's head and tilted it upside down to reveal an array of unoccupied inputs, plugging the connection for the mandibles into one of them. She placed him back down, making sure to run the mandibles out to his front.

They hung limp for a few moments and Eve second-guessed if they were even functional for a moment. The mandibles suddenly whirred to life and whipped upright, then left, then right. Spud clacked them together, thrusting their stumpy hydraulic arms in and out while he eyed the mandibles with keen curiosity. Eve could not help but snicker at Spud's experimentation with his new limbs. He rotated his optics onto her and responded with a beep and a few metallic claps of his mandibles.

'You're a pro already,' she said, her chest filling with pride.

Spud waved the mandibles around wildly, gratified that his limitations were now pushed beyond the realms of software. His head rocked back and forth in his manic thrashings and he toppled off his pile and rolled across the workbench, colliding with the idle computer monitor. The impact itself was not noteworthy, but it had enough force to rattle the monitor. Debris rained and peppered Spud's head. He booped in complaint under the deluge and brushed away stray components and cables off of him. A small piece of parchment caught his attention.

He beeped, reaching in vain for the parchment with a mandible. One of its fingers dug into it, and he dragged it close enough to where the second mandible scooped it up and held it before his optics for analysis. He scanned the thin paper, perhaps perplexed by its nature.

'That's just a photo, Spud,' Eve explained, standing Spud's head upright.

Spud beeped quizzically.

'That's my family,' Eve said, pointing to her clone on the parchment. 'That's me when I was little. I've grown up a fair bit since then, though.'

Spud booped, and Eve took it as a sign to continue.

'That's my mom and dad,' she added, tapping a finger against the last two remaining figures. 'They're my parents. Kinda like *my* creators.'

The word 'creator' struck Eve as strange coming out of her mouth, but she doubted Spud was able to comprehend anything else. She reached down and pinched a corner of the photograph, giving it a tug. Spud tugged back.

'It's okay, buddy,' she consoled. 'I just want to give it a quick look.'

He relinquished control and watched it float up out of reach.

Eve glanced at the photograph and felt a pang of envy. *So happy,* she thought, her bottom lip pushed out. *I want it back.* She leaned back and cast her gaze out the window. The

Rocket lay dormant at the fringes of her vision, the darkness almost swallowing it whole.

Perhaps I should talk to Mom? she thought. She had considered remaining in the common room, hoping to catch her mother upon her eventual return inside to ask her about the Rocket, but decided against it and instead retreated back into her room. *I shouldn't have even been out there to begin with,* she had told herself. *I probably only made things worse for myself.*

The tell-tale sound of the medbay door being opened made Eve freeze. She listened intently as footsteps trailed their way out into the common room and stopped before her door. There were a few moments of silence until some keys were pressed and an approving bleep answered. The door grinded open, and Nisma stood on the other side.

The stark contrast in light between her daughter's room and the common room cast her in a black silhouette that hid whatever expression she had on her face. 'Eve?' she said, brushing some hair out of her face. 'Can I come in?' Her tone was passive, devoid of any real sense of emotion.

A tougher scrutiny of her face revealed baggy eyes that overflowed with defeat and fatigue. The sorry state of her mother made Eve feel a wrench of pity. She nodded. 'Yeah. Yeah, you can come in.' She rose to her feet, leaving the photograph on the workbench.

Nisma shuffled her way in, leaning heavily against the wall. Eve could tell she was at the brink of falling over and offered up her chair. Nisma took it graciously and collapsed down into it with a huff. She sat there for a few moments, rubbing her face with her hands. Eve could see her mother more clearly now. She was a complete mess and was covered in sweat and grime from head to toe. If Eve did not know any better, she would have thought she had rolled around in the dirt outside.

Eve stood beside the chair, waiting for her mother to say something. Anything. 'Mom?' she asked, leaning down a bit to get a better look at her mother's face. 'Are you okay?'

Nisma sniffed, and Eve caught a fleeting glimpse of tears welling behind her mother's hands. *Is she crying?*

'Mom?' she asked again, laying a hand on Nisma's shoulder.

Nisma gripped Eve's hand with her own, unveiling a sodden wreck of a face. She sniffled and spluttered, her eyes and skin a shade of red. The sight hit Eve like a storm, and she fought back tears of her own. *She* is *crying.*

'I'm sorry, Eve,' her mother choked, not daring to make eye contact. 'I'm sorry for everything. I only wanted to keep you safe.'

Eve listened, no words coming to mind. She had spent a lot of her time locked in her room thinking of all manner of things to say to her mother; things born in anger and in spite, things designed to hurt someone at their very core. But when the time came for them to be unleashed and Eve finally locked eyes with her mother in a moment of stillness, nothing surfaced. All that she could think of was her mother who was now breaking down before her with no contribution from her whatsoever. It shook Eve to her very core. It made her feel sick for ever conceiving of such nasty things to say. It made her want to do one thing: make her mother feel better.

She knew there was only one thing to say. Eve swallowed, the words getting lodged in her throat for a second. 'I forgive you, Mom.'

'What?' Nisma said, looking up at her daughter with teary eyes. 'You do?'

Eve gave a stiff nod. 'I do. I'm sorry as well. For going out on my own. For getting Dad injured. For what I said to you.'

'It's okay.' Nisma smiled, kissing Eve's hand on her shoulder. 'Thank you.'

Eve returned the smile and leaned onto her mother's shoulder, resting her head against Nisma's. She felt grimy and smelt like she had not bathed in cycles, but Eve did not care. As far as she was concerned, she just wanted to hug her mom. There was a long moment of silence where neither Eve nor Nisma made any move. Eve relished the pause and hoped that the moment never ended.

'That damned Rocket' Nisma sighed, her mind always in motion. 'If it weren't for you, I doubt it would still be in one piece.'

Eve opened her eyes and saw Nisma had cast her gaze outside where the dim silhouette of the Rocket stood vigil.

'Tell me,' Nisma asked, turning to Eve. 'I made my software lockdown to be impossible to override. How did you break it so quickly?'

Eve blinked, taking a moment to process the question. 'Oh, it wasn't me. Spud opened it.'

Nisma raised an eyebrow. 'Spud?'

Spud beeped in acknowledgment.

Eve watched her mother's eyes widen in disbelief. '*That* opened the door?' she inquired, nodding towards the robotic head.

'*He* did. Yes,' Eve confirmed, not taking too kindly to her mother's use of words.

Nisma leaned forwards to get a better look of him. '*This* can integrate with the Rover's systems? How?' She picked up the head and examined it with unbridled curiosity.

Eve shrugged, keeping an eye on her mother's grip on Spud in case she risked dropping him. 'I don't know. I had only just gotten him working when the Rocket started exploding, and when I couldn't open the door, he did.'

Spud booped and waved his mandibles around, trying to grasp Nisma's face for a feel.

Nisma laughed, keeping him at arm's length. '*You* made this?'

Spud beeped in annoyance and consigned to pinching at Nisma's arms.

Eve nodded. A growing sense of pride welled inside her. She had never thought her mother would approve of Spud, let alone like him. Nisma had always said that the time and effort she put into him was a waste. Eve was thankful that it was no longer the case.

'It's incredible!' Nisma praised as she plucked Spud's mandibles from her arms.

'*He's* incredible,' Eve corrected again.

Nisma gave a mildly annoyed look at her daughter and laid Spud down atop his mountain. As her arms rose away from his head, Spud reached for one last pinch before retracting his mandibles and letting them sit idle by his side.

'Well, at least one of us is having success with their project.' Nisma sighed.

Eve sat down on the workbench and faced her mother. 'What happened?'

'I did some diagnostics after you left, at least what little I could without power,' Nisma explained, eyes growing dark. 'When you pulled that capacitor out to shut the Rocket down, it sent a large burst of energy back into the cores. They're all fried.'

'Oh,' Eve grumbled, averting her gaze. 'What now?'

'I don't know,' Nisma shrugged, scratching her cheek. 'The *Eternity* is gone, so there's no hope of getting more. I'm at a loss, and there's only fifty-two hours, thirty-four minutes until we *need* to launch.'

A burst of colours poured out from the processor unit within Spud's body, forcing Eve and Nisma to avert their eyes. The monitor to Eve's computer powered on, and window after window popped up and vanished as a foreign power took control.

'What's happening?' Nisma asked, peeking from between her fingers.

'I don't know,' Eve answered, anxious of what Spud was up to. 'But this is exactly what happened when Spud opened the door for me.'

'What's he doing?'

The monitor navigated through schematics, data records and information hubs before settling on a list of files, all sorted neatly in one window.

Nisma read the title of the window and gasped. 'These are Rover components!'

A new window opened up, showing a digital render of a large complex device laden with tubes, cables and wires.

'That's the Rover's reactor!' Nisma exclaimed, her eyes lighting up. 'There's still hope!'

'The Rover's reactor?' Eli asked, arms crossed. 'You certain?' He sat at his position at the dining table, leaning awkwardly to the side to keep pressure off of his leg. Nisma had finally given him the green light to leave the medbay, and he now waddled about the Rover in his newfound freedom with a crutch under his arm. He shot the occasional glance to Spud and could not help but smile at what his daughter managed to achieve with nothing but scraps and her wit.

Nisma could not agree more with him, and with the little robot's latest discovery, there may still be a chance to escape Concord. *And give her the life she deserves,* Nisma thought with a smile. *Eve deserves better than this.*

'Its output is *more* than enough for the thrusters, *and* it's lighter than the cores!' she explained, waving her hands around like it was a sales pitch.

She paced back and forth behind her chair, bubbling with a mix of excitement and anxiety. Her eyes bounced between Eli and her watch. She felt much better than before, having emerged from her bedroom a few minutes prior following a long rest. It was not without protest, of course, and it took a lengthy argument with both Eli and Eve before she bowed her knee, cleaned herself up and got some sleep. She initially doubted she could have even closed her eyes with all the excitement, but the moment her head touched the pillow, she passed out and did not stir for another thirteen hours.

Nisma waved to Eve. 'Isn't that, right?'

Eve nodded. She sat in her seat with her arms in her lap, watching her mother walk back and forth in her obsessive manner. She had remained silent for the most part, though she did make the occasional interjection to clarify matters when the subject shifted towards Spud.

Spud lay before her, his androgynous mass consuming a large portion of the table. He looked around, taking in the atmosphere with what Nisma assumed to be delight, occasionally emitting a boop to show his satisfaction. He initially showed great interest in Eli and had even managed to engage in a conversation with him, although it mainly consisted of Eli playing along with his monotonous bloops.

'Will it even fit?' Eli asked.

'With the cores and their supporting elements removed, there'll be plenty of space,' Nisma answered confidently.

Eli nodded, though he was evidently not entirely convinced. He sighed and rubbed his chin, a stubble having thoroughly settled in. 'Nis, if we remove the core, we *won't* be able to put it back in. We'll be on the backup batteries, which gives us little more than a cycle at best. *That's* if the air can last that long.'

Nisma was aware that it was a big proposition—and one that could have devastating effects if things went wrong—but with no alternatives left, it was the best chance they had at getting off world. She crossed her arms, and a small grin creeped at the edge of her mouth. 'The Satellite will be in position well before then. We'll be gone before that becomes an issue.'

Eli sighed again and took a moment to think. He eventually shrugged. 'Well, with the *Eternity* gone and my leg…gone, we're already on borrowed time.' His face went stern. 'You *need* to get that Rocket working, Nis.'

The schematics for the Rover contained a footnote which detailed its intentional design as merely a temporary solution for transportation in a potentially hostile extra-terrestrial environment, its functioning lifespan not expected to surpass a few months. It was never meant to be used as a permanent home and most certainly was not supposed to be disassembled. It was merely to be exploited then thrown away once its use had been spent.

Nisma knew this, and she wished there was another way about it. But it had to be done. *Maybe they'll let us come back down to recover it?* she had thought to herself. *Would they be generous enough to give us that?* She doubted it; it was just an ancient, rusted machine that worked solely on stubbornness and perseverance. But that did not stop Nisma from holding onto a smidgeon of hope.

When the panelling that contained the reactor was exposed, she had a momentary pulse of sadness wash through her at the sight. The Rover had served dutifully as the home for herself and her family for almost a decade, working in the worst conditions known to mankind and still having more to give. Now, it had given its heart over to them in one final act of servitude to them. The emotional lapse was brief, and Nisma pushed it away to put on a more focused demeanour. *Now's not the time for sentiment.*

The procedure was risky, and one wrong move during the entire extraction and subsequent installation process could have had terrible implications, if not for the reactor than most certainly for those around it. During the entire process, Nisma kept an eye on her watch for the time and an ear out for the Geiger counter in her pocket. Its idle crackling did amp up a bit once the reactor was exposed and connected to the crane. The crane was loud, rusty and lacked almost all means of fine adjustments, but under Eli's steady hand and guidance from Nisma and Eve, the reactor was extracted and hoisted outside onto a trailer for transport.

The journey between the Rover and Rocket was quick, the Rover having been moved beside the Rocket and hooked up to it, ready to tow. Nisma and Eve, donning cold-weather gear, transferred to the Rocket and pulled the reactor up using a system of pulleys while Eli remained in the cargo bay to pack up the crane. The reactor was heavy, and Nisma doubted she could have done it alone, especially with Eli out of action. So, she was thankful she and her daughter had put their grievances behind them to focus on the task at hand.

The installation was quick and easy, Nisma and Eve's flashlights bounding back and forth inside the cockpit in their fervour. The old cores and their supporting components were removed and tossed out the Rocket's open door before the reactor was pushed in and connected. They then methodically traced the route of power from the reactor throughout the system, replacing or resetting any blown or tripped fuses and capacitors.

Spud was present as well, Eve leaving him in the co-pilot's seat so he could watch. He examined the entire process and would beep and clack his mandibles in response to the occasional chatter from Eve.

'All right, that should be the last one,' Nisma said, pulling her head out from under the pilot's controls. She turned to Eve, who was observing with patient interest beside her, and nodded.

Eve nodded back, approached the controls and pressed the power button. The cockpit flickered on and dozens of buttons flashed and glowed a magnificent array of colours. Nisma's eyes bounced between the pilot's monitor and the reactor behind her, ensuring everything was working as intended.

After a few moments, the Rocket completed its start-up sequence and entered its idle state. She leaned over the controls and tapped away at the console, opening up the digital display of the thrusters. The schematics popped up one by one, leading their respective states and theoretical thrust outputs. Nisma's heart soared as the two primary thrusters returned green readings. As their names suggested, the primary thrusters provided the majority of the propulsion in the Rocket. But in order for them to escape Concord's gravity, Nisma needed at least three of the five auxiliary thrusters to be operational.

The situation went south as soon as the first auxiliary thruster reading came in and, one by one, each thruster coloured themselves red on the digital display until all five were blood crimson. Nisma's heart plummeted through the floor. She felt like she had been struck in the face. *It can't be! Not all of them!* A grim realisation settled in over her. She had given everything she had, and it still was not enough. Her eyes flickered to Eve, who was struggling to get a look at the monitor. Nisma did not want her to see this. Not when there was no alternative. No hope of change. No hope of survival.

'Hey, Eve,' Nisma said, moving herself to block the monitor from Eve's gaze. 'It's nearing lunchtime. Could you go into the Rover and start preparing? I'll be in shortly.' Her tone was blunt, but a hint of sadness managed to seep in.

'Okay,' Eve replied cautiously.

'Take Spud with you,' Nisma added, hoping with all her heart that Eve had not seen how hopeless the situation had become.

Eve scooped Spud up and waddled out the doorway, leaving him on the floor of the Rocket for a moment while she descended the ladder before picking him back up and continuing on her way.

Spud's optics were locked on Nisma the entire time, and she gave him a fleeting glance before turning away from his piercing look. *Did he notice?* she thought. She listened to Eve's footsteps as they slowly dissipated into the dark, before dropping down into the pilot's seat. She held a hand to her brow and pressed her goggles against her skull. She had exhausted every avenue of approach, every means of achieving what she believed to be the ticket to their freedom. She had held out hope that things were not as bad as she thought and that perhaps by some miracle, everything had survived the malfunction and remained intact.

'You're an idiot,' she told herself. 'A complete, fucking idiot.' She glanced back at the reactor and listened to it hum in uncaring mechanical serenity. 'You doomed us all.'

CHAPTER TEN

A stiff breeze wafted over the Outlook, its jagged, stalwart shape cast in flickering oranges and yellows. The debris from the *Eternity*'s detonation had since stopped falling and now hundreds of spot fires raged across the rolling landscape, stretching out as far as the horizon and most likely further beyond, to consume what little remained of the pinnacle of human achievement. Minor hovered high in the sky, its scarred form drenching Concord with a bounty of light that helped to soften the harsh influence of the fires on the rocky outcrop. But it could do little to conceal the hellscape that was the former site of the great vessel.

Nisma looked out over the land, watching the flashes and pops that ravaged the wreck atop its mountaintop grave. Her hands were tucked under her armpits, and her knees rattled a bit as a gust of frigid wind blew past her. The telescope stood beside her and a bag beside that, beholden only by moonlight.

The Geiger counter in her pocket clicked an ominous tune of death, the levels far exceeding what would be safe for long-term exposure. Nisma could almost feel the radiation rain down upon her and rise up from the rock below to penetrate her very soul. Her thick cold weather layers would absorb most of the radiation, but her flesh would still be exposed to potentially lethal doses. It did not matter to Nisma anyway. As far as she was concerned, she and everyone else she cared for only had until the batteries in the Rover ran flat and the air went stale. They would be dead long before they would have had to worry about radiation sickness.

Having grown tired of watching the fireworks, Nisma turned to the telescope set up beside her and entered in the right adjustments for the solar system. As she did, she cast her mind back to her childhood—the countless lessons about Earth and the many cultures that existed on it, the pictures of great oceans, lush forests, sandy deserts and all other manner of wondrous biomes. They played through her mind like the slideshows they were presented on. *Home.*

She was so caught up in her train of thought that she could have sworn she saw a small blue orb float before the Sun in the telescope's eyepiece, a momentary glimpse at what waited for her in the universe above. But she knew it was a ridiculous prospect. The Earth was too small, and Concord was too far away.

Just out of reach, Nisma concluded, pulling back from the eyepiece.

Her hands fiddled with the knobs, entering in a new set of adjustments, before she returned her face to the eyepiece. The Satellite came into view, first a blurry blob then a crystal-clear shape after Nisma focused the eyepiece. It was much larger than normal, its orbit putting it almost directly above Nisma and her telescope. It would be only a few hours away from drifting into launch position. Nisma checked her watch to confirm the timing: thirty hours, forty-eight minutes.

She returned her eye to the sight. It was the best view she had ever beheld of the Satellite. Nisma could make out fine details on the space station: solar panels, tunnels that connected the sections together, even large reflective surfaces which Nisma assumed to be windows or maybe even hangar bays of some kind. She wondered if whoever lived up there ever looked down upon Concord and watched her, Eli and Eve go about their daily struggle for survival.

Were they studying us? What have they witnessed? Did they see the Eternity *explode?* These were all questions that had plagued Nisma's mind since she first sighted the celestial object years prior, floating gracefully high in orbit without a care for what happened below.

She had tried to raise contact with them to try and organise a means of rescue. But there was nothing. Nisma had exhausted every means of communication to the Satellite to no avail, the atmosphere not permitting any signals to flee into orbit. So, not keen on waiting for someone else to make the first move, she instead decided to build her own means to get to them.

'How's it looking?' an approaching voice inquired.

Nisma jumped, and she pulled away from the eyepiece. A beam of light weaved its way up from the cave, picking its path carefully. Nisma fumbled with her flashlight and turned it on, finding the person behind the opposing light to be Eli. Clad in cold-weather gear, mask, goggles and crutch under his shoulder, he waddled his way to Nisma's side.

Nisma rose to her feet. 'You shouldn't be outside.'

'Please,' Eli tutted. 'I think we're beyond caging each other up now, aren't we?'

Nisma lowered her gaze, annoyed at herself for falling into that trap again. 'Sorry.'

Eli stopped beside her, wobbling slightly as his weight shifted between his working leg and his crutch. He aimed his flashlight down and away from Nisma's face. She did the same.

He eyed off the telescope. 'What you looking at?'

Nisma motioned to the telescope and Eli took her invitation. He leaned down with great difficulty, but refused any offer
of help from Nisma. His eye lined up with the eyepiece, and he observed in silence for a few moments. 'Okay. I'll admit it.' He chuckled in his usual optimistic manner. 'It's definitely *not* a chunk of the moon.'

Nisma could not help but let a little snicker out. It always befuddled her how he managed to make her laugh. 'Glad you see things my way now,' she said with a smile, although she knew Eli could not see it.

Eli pulled away from the eyepiece and straightened up with a pained grunt, satisfied with his observation. His composure told Nisma that he had not simply marched out to the Outlook in the bitter cold just to do a bit of astronomy.

'What's wrong, Nis?' He sighed, leaning against his crutch.

Nisma raised an eyebrow. 'What do you mean?'

'You're not working,' Eli pointed out bluntly. 'We're at the eleventh hour and you're out here stargazing.'

Nisma bit her lip. She had not told him of the Rocket's failures yet. She did not know if she could stomach it. 'I just wanted to take a break.'

'You're a terrible liar, Nis,' Eli stated as soon as she finished, the words being held at an instant. 'What happened?'

Nisma grumbled, irritated by her husband's sharp nature. *There's no escaping it. Might as well come clean.*

She swallowed, the words fighting to stay in her mouth. 'The reactor works and we got a diagnostic from the thrusters,' she started, hoping to ease the impact with some good news as fruitless as it was. 'But almost all of the auxiliary thrusters are burnt out. I forgot to factor in *their* power intake limits when I did the test.'

Eli did not answer for a few moments, and Nisma felt every passing microsecond grind on like a lifetime. A fleeting gust of wind made them waver like the trees that used to inhabit Central Park.

'So, it's the death sentence then,' he concluded, looking out over the horizon at the *Eternity*. 'Does *she* know?'

'Eve?' Nisma said, shaking her head. 'I don't think so. I sent her inside before she could get a good look at the results. I've spent the last few hours trying to find a solution, anything, but there's nothing. There's nothing left.'

A surge of emotion boiled up from inside her, and she launched a mighty kick into the empty bag next to the telescope with a roar. The bag careened up a few metres before landing with a thump on the ground.

'Fuck!' she screamed, her tormented voice echoing across the barren nightscape. 'I screwed up, Eli. I fucked it! Fucked it royally!' She dropped to one knee and rubbed at teary eyes, immediately growing more furious at the goggles that blocked her hands. 'There aren't any other alternatives, Eli. There's nothing left.'

A bout of sniffles came from under her mask as the weight of her failure crashed down upon her. Eli's hand patted her shoulder firmly and Nisma felt her anguish ease at her husband's touch.

'Well, not exactly,' he said, rubbing Nisma's shoulder.

'What do you mean?' she asked between sniffles.

'You said just the auxiliary thrusters were blown out, right?' Eli asked. 'So, the primary thrusters still work?'

Nisma nodded, unsure of where Eli was going. 'Yeah, but we'll still be one hundred and twenty-six kilos overweight, and I've already scraped out as much excess weight as I could. We won't make it.'

'So, there's still one option left,' Eli said with a slight nod.

It took Nisma a second for the pieces to click in her head. She leapt to her feet and shook her head in disbelief at what Eli was proposing. 'Eli, no, we can't!' she exclaimed, marching up into Eli's face. 'I *won't* put her through it!'

Eli took a step back and shrugged. 'All the pieces are in play, Nis. It's your call.'

Spud was in his usual spot atop Eve's workbench. He watched as Eve fiddled with a device which he had determined to be a track system to serve as a basic form of locomotion for him. He was thankful that Eve worked so diligently to give him the upgrades and theorised whether her own creators also did the same for her. He concluded that they had, though the means by which had still eluded him.

Eve hummed as she worked, a smile on her face. Spud observed in silence. He doubted she knew how bad things really were. Her posture was too optimistic, too forward-thinking. He deliberated informing her of what he had seen in the Rocket. What Nisma had tried in vain to hide from her.

+*Do you really want to tell her of her imminent demise?*+ the Foreigner's presence said in its esoteric manner, a rare occurrence following Spud's initial start-up.

Spud could see the logic in the Foreigner's words. He, himself, did not wish to be terminated, and the very idea of knowing its proximity would have made it all the worse. His optics flickered momentarily over his creator. He did not know how a being like Eve could terminate. Would she simply shut down like he would? What would happen to her components and upgrades? Would they be recycled or disposed of? What was the expected usable lifetime of such a being? Was it even possible for them to cease function? Did she fear being shut down or was his anxiety just a weakness of his primitive alloyed brain?

There was still so much that Spud did not know about his creator, and he had developed countless theories on the mechanics of his creator by observing her mannerisms. She would engage in episodic rest periods at roughly the same time of every cycle, likely to preserve her battery life or even recharge it. She would also often ingest some forms of matter, which Spud theorised was probably an energy-rich substance used in chemical reactions. Perhaps it was *that* which kept her charged? These theories floated around in Spud's RAM constantly, but they remained little more than that.

He inquired the Foreigner for any input on the subject matters, but it was silent.

This disgruntled Spud. Was it ignoring him? Since his awakening, he had discovered the full extent of the integration of their two forms and had concluded that they were so intertwined they were practically inseparable. That realisation concerned Spud, because if the Foreigner was suddenly absent from his form, would he still be able to function? Or would he meet his termination? It was a rogue factor that he did not particularly relish.

Spud prodded the Foreigner for input again, but it remained stoic.

Spud disregarded the Foreigner and cast his optics around the workbench, stopping the instant he caught sight of the photograph leaning against the computer monitor a short distance away. He regarded the miniature clones of Eve and her parents with intrigue, and after casting a quick glance in Eve's direction to ensure she was not looking, he extended a mandible and pinched the corner of the photograph. He reeled in the photograph and beheld the scene it depicted.

A momentary spike of intrigue registered in him as he beheld the creators of *his* creator. He noted that both Eli and Nisma were considerably larger than Eve. Perhaps this was the largest size they upgraded to? But how could it be that something like Eve could change? She had no visible components, no seams between joints and no electrical discharge or static that Spud could detect, at least of a usable level. Whatever she was consisted of, it was of a completely different material and make up than what Spud was.

The question lingered: how did *she* change? His optics lowered to his mandibles under the photograph. Was it similar to how *he* was upgraded? Perhaps Eve underwent upgrades of her own, trading in old and insufficient components for newer, stronger, bigger ones? Perhaps she utilised some form of microscopic technology that grew her form as she matured? That was a viable proposition, but one that definitely strayed on the illogical by Spud's metrics. His theories garnered an overwhelming desire to keep the photograph for future study, but he knew that it must be done discreetly should he wish to avoid feeling the wrath of his creator.

The sound of the airlock activating brought Spud up out of his internal opinions. He reached out into the wireless network and connected into the camera system. Flicking through the list of viewpoints, he sighted Nisma doff several jackets and trail a route through the cargo bay, into the common room and up to Eve's door. Spud noted an irregularity in her composure—much less stable and confident than usual. He noticed several attempts to clean up her face with her sleeves and a prolonged dress correction in front of Eve's door. Had she come to tell Eve of what *he* could not?

Eve paused her work at the sound of knocking at her door. 'Come in,' she said, raising her head from the track system.

The door opened, and Nisma strolled in, a neutral look on her face. 'Can you go downstairs and help your father in the airlock?' she asked, voice wavering a little. 'I need to check on the state of the batteries.'

'Okay,' Eve acknowledged, rising and shuffling past Nisma.

Nisma remained in place and watched as Eve paced out into the common room and down the ladder.

While all eyes were focused elsewhere, Spud took his opportunity and folded up the photograph with both mandibles, taking care to not damage it, and opened a small disc tray in a data reader that lay on the side of his pile of auxiliary components. It was an obsolete platform, one that Spud could not fathom a purpose for at the present, so he relegated it to physical storage for the time being. He placed it onto the tray, ensuring no portion of it protruded outside of the circular depression, and closed it.

After a few moments, Nisma turned back and closed the door behind her. She glared at Spud, a look of determination on her face. 'I know you saw it,' she grumbled, marching up to the workbench and scooping Spud's head into her hands. 'The thrusters.'

Spud booped in confirmation, his optics meeting hers. He analysed them and found them to be red and considerably dilated. A clear fluid dripped down from them and was swiftly wiped away with her sleeve.

'Now, if what I've seen is true,' Nisma said sternly. 'You are far smarter than you would like to let on and are more than capable of achieving things that are more…technologically oriented.'

Spud acknowledged, although he could hardly claim credit
for it as whatever influence he has over technology was solely
the result of the other being that also inhabited his body.

+*On that matter, you would be correct,*+ the Foreigner
affirmed, seeming to rouse from its self-imposed silence.

Spud languished a little. He had grown comfortable
without the presence of the Foreigner in his head.

Spud saw a grin crack Nisma's mouth. 'That's what I
thought,' she said, laying Spud down and taking a seat in
Eve's chair. Her eyes locked with Spud's optics. 'I would like
to make a *very* important request of you. One that I *hope* you
would be willing to undertake.'

Eve worked at her computer until the very last minute,
making hurried modifications to Spud's software until the
final volt of electricity had been sapped from the Rover's
back-up battery and everything powered down for one last
time. She watched as the monitor burned out, and the
monotonous whirs from the computer droned into silence. Her
eyes lingered for a moment, staring at the blank monitor,
before the lights in her room finally dimmed for good. She
remained still for a moment, her mind elsewhere, until she
snapped back to reality and flicked on her brain.

'Sorry, buddy. That'll be all for now,' she said, unplugging
Spud.

He booped as she scooped him up, being careful to take up every rogue piece of him into her arms until he hefted against her chest like a pile of rocks.

Eve gave one fleeting glance at her workbench and realised just how big it was without Spud atop it. She looked at her bed, its form old and tired from years of abuse. Many nights of sleep—most were good, some were bad, others she wished she could forget. Eve never noticed how small it was, tucked away under the bunk like a cavity made for rodents. Her floor was still a mess, but it had become a normality for her at this point. She wished she could take it all, but was told that weight limitations meant she could only bring Spud along. She moved to turn, but her feet were stuck to the ground, forcing her eyes to record as much of her home as possible. She nodded, gloom seeping in. *My old home*

'Eve? You ready?' Nisma's voice hollered up from the cargo bay. 'It's time to go.'

'Coming,' Eve answered, taking one last look at her old life before passing through her open door and into the common room.

She navigated the ladder carefully and passed into the airlock where Nisma waited. Spud exchanged hands to Nisma while Eve donned her cold-weather gear. After sealing her goggles and purging her mask, Eve beckoned for Spud to be returned to her. Nisma obliged and activated the airlock override, initiating an opening through the use of the stored air that remained in its system—a backup feature, should it ever lose power. Eve was thankful the original designers had the foresight to include such a feature. *They really were forward thinking. I wonder how things are now?*

The airlock grinded open, needing a helpful shove from Nisma for the last few inches. They stepped out in a cloud of misty air and disturbed dirt. The Outlook loomed ahead, the Rover having been parked a short distance from the Rocket's launch site. At the rock formation's peak, the Rocket stood upright, tall and proud. Several floodlights bathed the Rocket and the surrounding ground in light.

The view left Eve breathless, and she had a fleeting sense of *déjà vu. Just like the nightmare,* she thought, concerned as she recollected the events that had led up to her fictitious death. She shook the thought away, convincing herself that her concerns were unfounded. *This is nothing like that. Now's not the time to worry.*

Nisma led Eve along a set of Rover tracks towards the Rocket. They climbed and climbed, making the occasional detour to avoid upturned boulders and fallen rubble until they were level with the Rocket.

Above them the sky was its typical starry self, and Eve tried to pick out which star was the Sun. Minor hung midway up the sky, its scarred form unleashing a deluge of silvery light that almost made the floodlights unnecessary. Its fragments held their position around the celestial body, frozen in time in the moment of whatever calamity had ridden them aeons ago. Flashes of light streaked across the sky as yet more debris rained down upon Concord as it usually did, thankfully landing several thousand kilometres to the west in the sunny side of Concord. Eve watched warily and wondered if any of those chunks of matter that moved at such astronomical speeds were remnants of the *Eternity*.

'Hey, Eevee,' Eli called out as he emerged from behind the Rocket. 'Ready to go?'

'Sure am,' Eve called back, a big smile on her face.

'Atta girl,' Eli cheered, rubbing his hand rigorously through Eve's hair when she stopped before him.

The instant Eli was finished with Eve, Nisma dropped to her knees and wrapped her up in a tight embrace. A few muffled sniffles seeped out from under her mask. Eve tried to breathe as best she could as her guts were crushed inside her mother's hug. Her hands floundered with Spud, and she almost dropped him in the dirt. A few painful moments passed, and she squirmed against her mother's grasp, grunting and groaning in protest.

Eventually, the stranglehold that had befell Eve loosened, though whether by her complaints or of Nisma's own volition was up for debate, and Eve wiggled herself free. Nisma's arms were held out for a moment, as if her mind was on a second's delay before she sheepishly retracted them and rose to her feet. It all confused Eve, and she developed mixed feelings about what had just happened. She looked up to Nisma for some form of hint, but her mother swiftly turned her head away, looking off at some unknown distant object.

'Here, Eevee,' Eli said, kneeling down and holding out a radio earpiece for her. 'It's gonna be a bit hard to hear each other when we launch so put this on.'

'Okay.' Eve nodded, slipping the earpiece in and connecting it to her wrist computer.

Eli straightened up and gave an unusually stiff nod. 'Good girl. Better get on board. Your mother and I just need to check a few things.'

Eve nodded and skipped over to the Rocket with Spud in hand. The climb up into the Rocket was much more difficult than when it was laid down in the cave, but after tossing Spud up into the cockpit and using several extruding pipes and bars as leverage, Eve managed to haul herself in. The reorientated cockpit caught her off guard for a moment, the rear panelling that housed the reactor becoming the floor and the chairs were built into a wall, looking up into the sky at least a metre and a half off the floor.

Eve scooped Spud back up into her arms, and on the tips of her toes, she reached up and dropped him into the passenger seat, the lowest of the seats. She followed soon after, heaving herself up with great difficulty. A lengthy game of musical chairs played out as Eve danced around with Spud's fluidlike body until he lay against her lap and stomach with his head level with her chest.

She sat awkwardly in the seat, her head a solid half foot below the headpiece and her knees just barely reaching the seat's front edge to allow her feet to dangle. She wiggled to get a better groove for the chair, but decided to accept her inadequacies. Her hands reached up and excised a pair of straps from the chair's shoulders. She pulled them down to her waist where, after some rearrangement with Spud, she plugged them into a central node that fastened her firmly in place.

A burst of static crossed Eve's earpiece, followed by Eli's voice. 'You got me, Eevee?'

'Yep,' Eve nodded, looking up out the windscreen at the starry sky. She wondered what might be different once they had left Concord, the marvellous things beyond her comprehension. She wanted to see Earth most of all, to witness what her mother had described to her and see the trees that her father led her to.

'Seatbelt on? Eli asked in Eve's ear.

'Yep,' Eve confirmed, checking her seatbelt was tight.

'Spud safe?'

'Yep.'

Spud gave a boop to show his acknowledgment.

'Awesome…' Eli said apprehensively.

His tone struck Eve as strange, much like Nisma's demeanour. She waited for a follow up, but there was nothing. Eve craned her head to get a view out the door and noticed that Eli and Nisma had barely moved since she left them. They both just stood there by each other's sides, silent and still like shadows.

There was a crackle in Eve's ear as Eli fumbled with the radio. 'Eve?' His tone was grim.

It did not sit well with Eve. She was hesitant to respond. 'Yeah?'

A moment of quiet.

'We're really sorry.'

Spud booped, and the necklace lit up in a flurry of colours.

In an instant, the Rocket had turned itself on and the door slammed shut with a violent hiss as the atmospheric seals engaged. The pilot's console fired up, and the array of buttons and levers burst into their spectacle of colours and noises.

'What's happening?!' Eve screamed, panic setting in. 'Mom?! Dad?!' She ripped at her seatbelt, but it refused to budge. 'My seatbelt is stuck!'

Spud beeped in acknowledgment, and the pieces fell into place.

Eve grabbed his head and glared at him dead in the optics. 'Spud?! What are you doing?! Let me out! Open the door!' He did not answer, his optics remaining enigmatic regardless of her demands.

Eve dropped his head and whipped around in her seat, hoping to find a small crevice that she could squeeze through. It was fruitless, and she turned back to the door where she could see out the small observation window. Eli and Nisma were still visible, their forms having grown smaller as they retreated to a safe distance.

'Mom! Dad! Help me!' Eve begged, tears starting to flow from her eyes.

The Rocket jolted as the thrusters finished their ignition sequences, their dull droning filling the Rocket with white noise. Eve could feel the Rocket teeter at the brink of launch and knew that time was running out for it to be stopped.

'NO! STOP! PLEASE!' she cried at the top of her lungs, ripping at the seatbelt again.

'This was the only way, Eve,' Nisma's voice said in her ear, wavering at the precipice of breakdown.

'Mom?' Eve said, unsure of what to make of her words.

'You don't belong here,' Nisma continued between bouts of sniffs and coughs. 'You belong up there, where you can flourish and become the best person you can be.'

Eve shook her head, not believing what she was hearing. 'No! No, don't go!'

'Hold your head high, kiddo,' Eli added, voice shaky as well. 'It's only up from here.'

'I don't want to go,' Eve sobbed, coughing into her mask. 'Don't leave me!'

There was a moment of silence before the radio activated again.

'We love you, Eve,' Nisma said, wholeheartedly.

Eve stammered, 'Mommy…'

'And don't you ever forget that,' Eli added.

'Daddy…'

The Rocket lurched and leapt up into the sky before Eve could muster anything else to say. Her lungs were crushed as Spud's mass grew in magnitudes under g-forces. The sky before her surged forwards as if the Rocket was plummeting into an ocean of stars. Eve tried to scream, but her voice got stuck in her throat. She coughed and spluttered, fighting to get a single breath into her lungs. Her heart thumped in her head, and a warm streak traced down her brow as her blood pressure reopened her Mark of *Eternity*.

After a fraction of a minute, though for Eve it felt like an eternity, the sky darkened and sounds dulled. Eve could not tell whether she was in space or her brain was giving its last hurrah. For a moment, she thought she could see a distant object that soon developed shape and form. She could feel herself growing lightheaded, and she fought to keep her eyes open, but it was a losing battle. Her mind grew foggy, and she soon succumbed to unconsciousness.

Her last thoughts were of Concord, the Rover, the *Eternity* and her parents.

WHAT TO READ NEXT

THE SECOND BOOK IN THE MARK OF ETERNITY SERIES

CHILD of CONCORD

ZACHARY MOULDER

The second instalment of the Mark of Eternity series!

She escaped eternal night only to find an even darker universe.

Six years have passed since Eve fled the smothering darkness of Concord Prime. At odds with a galaxy under the heel of the Coalition, she finds solace in building her robotic son, Spud, alongside various devices for her adoptive father and avid collector of relics from humanity's past, Vaughn.

But when a being from an age long forgotten reveals itself to her, the fate of the universe is thrust into her palm. With the ghosts of her past haunting every shadow, the true colours of those she holds dear coming to light, and a piece of the Eternity being the key to it all, Eve is forced to make a choice.

Will she sacrifice what little light she has left? Or will she let the universe die?

A FRIENDLY REMINDER

How did you find Mark of Eternity? Please leave a review!
Good or bad, I'm keen to see what you think.

Spot any mistakes? Let me know! I'm run a one-man
operation so it's inevitable for mistakes to slip through.

Want to remain up to date with any future works? Check out
my socials that I frequent every so often. If you're interested
in receiving an Advanced Reader Copy for future works, then
keep an eye out on there.

Twitter: @ZacMoulder
Email: zachary.d.moulder@gmail.com

AFTERWORD

Well, welcome to the end. I thoroughly hope you enjoyed reading this little piece of literature that has plagued my mind, both waking and sleeping, for the past two years. It was a long trudge through writer's block, innumerable re-writes, a few shelvings and even a flip-flop or two between formats and genres. But now it's finally finished and in a state that I'm confident enough to call my first finished story.

I first got the inspiration for Mark of Eternity while watching a certain sci-fi movie involving killer aliens. In fact, the very scene that inspired it happens at the beginning where a family drives a very Rover-esque vehicle through the rain on a distant planet. Funny how that happens. The rest I've plucked from fiction, non-fiction and my own experiences.

I've been writing dips and dabs for almost ten years by the time MoE is released and I have dozens of stories floating around in my head all fighting for supremacy and my attention. This happened for a long time until I had finally grown tired of bouncing between works, changing my vibe and inevitably hitting a wall before restarting the whole process again. So, I decided to clamp down on one story and see it through to the end, no matter how long it might take.

It just so happens that Mark of Eternity (which I had nicknamed Scavenger at the time) was the closest to completion. It was also an absolute trainwreck. I had initially set out on MoE with the intent of making it a novel, but I decided to switch to a comic format to appeal to another audience. I had gotten the script written up and the story was good to go. All I had to do was illustrate it. However, noting that I cannot draw to save my life, I had to look to freelancers for the work. Most artists declined or straight up ignored my offers and those that did respond ended up making works that were well below my expectations (not that they were bad, I just wanted MoE to be the best it can be). So, after a while of contemplation, I decided to return to the novel format and a few months of vicious writing followed.

Once I had finished the novel draft, I found my copyeditor, C.K. Korfo (ck_korfo), on Fiverr and gave him the first few thousand words of MoE. I was anxious, I had never let anyone outside of family read my work and I thought it would get ripped apart and thrown to the wind. My life's dream would have likely ended right then and there if that happened. But when C.K. responded, it was a massive relief. He thoroughly liked it, and aside from some minor spelling and grammar corrections, he only had one issue; the POV. It was a remnant of MoE's infancy as a comic book. I had written it in an omniscient narration, bounding between characters with no rhyme or reason. I tried to stick by it even after C.K.'s suggestion to change to a limited POV, but I soon realised that I must do what was best for the story, not my stubbornness. So, I made the changes and the story's flow smoothened out. It was a finished book, the first I had ever even come close to. It was special to me, but I also wanted to make it special for the reader.

The books I normally read often contain little illustrations of characters or action scenes scattered throughout them. They were sparse, often only a handful each novel, but they did serve as a nice refresh point even if their crude formatting hinted to their inclusion as more of an afterthought than a proper part of the work. I wanted my story to have pictures, too, but with a deliberate styling choice to really help them meld with the story and make the finished product better than the sum of its parts. Doan Trang (doantrang on Fiverr) was particularly helpful with this. Her monochromatic style was exactly what I was looking for and it matched the dark (both literally and symbolically) tone of MoE perfectly.

As for characters and the story itself, it did not really change. Some sections were shuffled around as POV and formats were altered but for the most part, everything stayed the same. The most glaring piece I can think of was Eli and Nisma's views on the Rocket. Initially, I had them reversed! Crazy now that I think back on it and it definitely did not settle well with their characters. Their personalities stayed the same, but they also had some sprinklings of mental disorder sewn in. Eli used to have bouts of bi-polar but I removed it because it made him seem too antagonising. Nisma still has a bit of her OCD, but it never really was a particularly extroverted feature of her personality so I never sought to change it. Eve was always the same; the naïve girl who loved her parents and only wanted a friend. That friend being Spud, who's inspiration came from a character I played in a tabletop game by the same name. Then there's the Foreigner. It was a late addition, something to give the necklace a bit of perspective. It was always present in the story, but with the Foreigner, I was now able to give its thoughts a voice and help work its relationship with Spud a bit better.

And this is the result. It's not perfect and there's several annoying titbits that still bug me to this day but I'll bite the bullet and learn to live with it. Needless to say, I will definitely be doing things different in the future (like not writing a damn comic book first) and I'm already well underway with my next story. It's not a sequel (though I definitely have another story in mind for our characters in MoE) but it is set in the same universe. I aim to eventually create a whole network of characters and events that interact and influence each other in a constantly evolving and living galaxy. Get keen for that, I know I am.

Anyway, for someone who doesn't normally like to talk much about anything, I've managed to spit out several pages worth of nonsense. I won't hold you hostage any longer.

Until next time,

Zachary Moulder

ΛBOUT THE ΛUTHOR

Zachary Moulder is an average bloke who likes to write
stories, paint very small miniatures and enjoy the company of
his friends and family over a few beers. Formerly an M1A1
Abrams Crewman, he is now an Ammunition Technician
serving in the Australian Army. He was born in Brisbane,
Australia, and presently resides in Townsville where he lives
in constant dread for the inevitable arrival of North
Queensland's insufferable summer.

www.ingramcontent.com/pod-product-compliance
Lightning Source LLC
Chambersburg PA
CBHW022156170626
46807CB00005B/2235